The Green Gene

PETER DICKINSON

THE
GREEN GENE

PANTHEON BOOKS
A Division of Random House, New York

Library of Congress Cataloging in Publication Data

Dickinson, Peter, 1927–
The Green Gene.

  I. Title.
PZ4.D5525Gr3 [PR6054.I35]   823'.9'14   72-12857
ISBN 0-394-48542-4

Manufactured in the United States of America

3   5   7   9   8   6   4   2

First American Edition

PART I

Whiteside

I

Replying to the debate the Home Secretary said, amid cheers, that nothing was more obnoxious to the people of Britain than racial discrimination. Every citizen of this country, as well as every foreign visitor, was issued with a National Health Card. This card entitled him to many benefits, chief among which was that in its top right-hand corner it carried an absolutely clear statement of the owner's racial status. If the card read 'Saxon' and any-one—anyone whatsoever, Cabinet Minister or petty offi-cial—attempted to treat the owner as other than a Saxon, then the severest penalties of the law could be visited on him. It made no difference whether the owner was black or brown or yellow or white; he was entitled to all the protection of Saxon Law. And the same thing, mutatis mutandis, *applied to Celts and the Celtic Law. It was an irrelevance that the majority of Celts, and no Saxons, had green skins. That was a genetic accident. Celtic Law had come down to us from very ancient origins, via the ancient Brehon laws of Ireland and the more modern mysteries of Scots Law.* (Some laughter.) *Its very survival proved that Celtic Law was peculiarly suited to the Celtic culture and temperament. It was in no sense dis-crimination to apply to people the law that most suited them. In fact, under new regulations which he proposed shortly to lay before Parliament, anyone who suggested that this was racial discrimination would automatically become guilty of incitement to racial hatred, and follow-ing an appearance before the Race Relations Tribunal,*

7

would be sentenced to a minimum of five years in a
Conciliation Camp. (Cheers.)

The Home Secretary was about to continue his speech
when the Speaker adjourned the debate to allow the
Chamber to be searched for an explosive device. ('Bomb
Threat in Parliament': see page 2, col. 4.)

P. P. Humayan lowered his suitcase to the pavement.
Almost he sat on it, but then recalled that people who sit
on suitcases in public are riff-raff, exiles, undocumented
wanderers silted into the transit areas of airports; where-
as he, P. P. Humayan, had all his papers in order and
a definite destination. Well, almost definite—there was
something about Doctor Glister's letter that left him a
little uneasy. And anyway, if he sat on the suitcase its
strained and ancient clasp would probably burst.

So he stood to rest, breathing the fumy May air, and
watched a municipal street-sweeper working his way up
the gutter of the tree-lined avenue, a gaunt and defeated
figure who leaned on his brush as much as he swept
with it; the pile of dust and lolly-wrappers became no
larger as it was nudged along the gutter because the
sweeper's technique shed precisely the same amount of
litter as he gathered. But he was very picturesque,
framed under the plane-trees with his dark uniform setting off the brilliant green of his face and hands. For
the first time Humayan understood a mystery that had
always interested him, why tourists in his native Bombay
had spent so much good film photographing beggars and
outcasts. Here, now, in London, if his own camera had
been working he might well have taken a photograph
of this sweeper to send home to his mother. A colour
photograph. He could afford that now.

A fat white Mercedes slid into the kerb, hooting at the
sweeper to jump clear and scattering the hoarded pile
of litter as he did so. Nine Chinese in sharply cut light-
weight suits popped out, shook hands energetically with
each other and strutted into a bar called McWatter's
Auld Bothie, Saxons only. Their chauffeur hooted again
and slid the car away; he too was green. The sweeper
fetched his cart and shovelled a fresh pile of dust and

8

litter out of it into the gutter; he gathered to it the larger remnants of his previous pile and swept the whole mess slowly on.

Typical, thought Humayan. But he was comforted, as one always is in a strange country when one's preconceptions about its inhabitants are confirmed.

Two policemen came round the corner by the dry-cleaner, blue-eyed, pink-cheeked, dark-moustached, walking with a curious weighty stroll as though it were part of their duties to tread the paving-stones more firmly into position. Their blue stare flicked along the avenue and rested on Humayan. His whole body seemed to gulp, once. He was perfectly entitled to be here, perfectly entitled—but he felt very small and very dark-skinned in this zone of pink giants. His left hand made a snatching movement towards his breast pocket, and then deliberately he drew out Doctor Glister's letter and sketch-map. He would ask them the way, and only show them his Card when they demanded to see it.

The avenue seemed to shrink into stillness at their coming. But when they were five paces away the stillness moved. It was nothing you could call a sound—more a sudden shuffling of the air, caused by some large disturbance several miles away. The policemen glanced at each other, swung aside and moved up the avenue at a pace that was almost hurried. Humayan's relief as he watched them go was mixed with gratification. No revolvers flopped against their buttocks, so this must be an area where the police still walked unarmed, a very superior residential district, in fact. Since he had the sketch-map out, he checked it again. The last landmark would be a pub.

The pub was a glaring white building, picked out with shiny black, but quite old. It looked as though the brewers who owned it had decided to keep its crumbling plaster in place with a carapace of fresh paint. Beside it ran a cobbled alley; the name-plate on the wall said 'Horseman's Yard'; he was there.

Disappointment washed through him. He thought of the shouts from the drinkers in the evenings, the picric

9

reek of old drinks in the mornings. What sort of doctor lived down a shabby alley behind a place such as this? If there was an outside lavatory he would not stay. On the other hand Doctor Glister's writing-paper had been thick and crisp, and the address elegantly printed. With a sigh of uncertainty Humayan lugged his suitcase into the alley. The beer-smell was strong but tolerable.

The alley was barred at the end by a wrought-iron screen with a gate in it. Twirly metal letters spelt out the words 'This Yard is Private Property'. Beyond the screen he could see hanging baskets of blue and scarlet flowers, their colours vivid against new purple brick and big sheets of glass and strips of aluminium. The gate was not locked but when he opened it a mellow buzzer sounded and several dogs started to bark. He saw at once that he had been wrong. The Yard was a very superior place, very superior indeed.

The paving was variegated with patches of round black pebbles set into cement; the eight houses had the crisp lines of total newness. The architect had managed to fit in touches that suggested these were artists' studios, but it was clear that only rich, young, smart, reliable artists would feel at home here. A green maid with blazing orange hair was polishing the windows of Number Two. With that elated feeling that Humayan knew from experience meant that the planets were combining to favour him, he strode to the door of Number Six and pressed the bell. Its tenor fluting was drowned in a flurry of barks. A ghost shape formed beyond the pearled glass of the door and hunched to peer at him through the spyhole; this was set a little high for someone of his stature, so he stood back to allow himself to be clearly seen. He felt beautifully confident. A blonde girl opened the door.

"We're all atheists," she said, "and we've got enough kitchen spatulas."

She spoke as though both bits of news were enormously cheering. She was younger than he had expected.

"Mrs. Glister?" he said.

"Christ, no!"

She had in fact made a movement as if to close the door, but now she stood still.

"My name is P. P. Humayan. I have received a letter from Doctor Glister inviting me to be his lodger in a room which he says is vacant at this address."

"Christ!"

They stood staring at each other for a while. Humayan's confidence was still effervescing all through him, and fizzed all the more in the presence of this clean, pink, pretty girl. Her fair hair had been through the curlers and was a shock of bright fuzz; she wore a maroon T-shirt and wide-legged maroon trousers; her flesh looked not soft but resilient, as though when you pressed it you would find it supple and springy. He licked mental lips and wondered whether she had a lover.

"Christ," she said, resignedly this time. "Does Mum know?"

"Doctor Glister's letter says 'My wife and I will be happy to welcome you...'" said Humayan, pulling the letter out and handing it across, wishing that it wasn't now so grubby with reperusal. She read it frowning, then looked quickly round Horseman's Yard.

"If Mrs. Glister..." began Humayan.

"Oh, she knew someone was going to have Moirag's room. I mean, that was her idea, but ... I mean ... does she know about ... Christ, I suppose you'd better come in. Mum's taking Glenda to the dentist. I suppose I'd better give Dad a ring. Christ. I suppose you'd better leave your bag in the hall for the moment."

The hall was close-carpeted in soft gold. The living room, whose big plate window looked across the Yard, smelt of rich sweet tobacco but was otherwise aseptic, with bleak abstracts on the walls and low, square-cornered furniture. A complex record-player extruded a pother of gibbering drums. Two curious small dogs, like tail-less squirrels, yelped at Humayan until the girl threw cushions at them when they slunk under a coffee table and began to lick their sexual organs. She turned the drummer off and sighed.

"I apologise for the confusion," said Humayan. "I came very precipitately, because I have a friend in Air India

11

who, you know, sometimes has very cheap tickets to sell
—but only at the last minute. I explained this to your
father, that I couldn't be sure of the date, and he said,
you see, it was OK. But even so I apologise..."

She cut him short with a sigh, picked up the telephone,
dialled two digits and paused.

"Look, Mr. ... er..."

"Humayan."

"That's right. I mean does he know ... I mean do
you know about our, you know, zoning laws? I mean..."

Humayan took out his wallet and worked his National
Health Card free. He took it across to the girl and
showed her the essential word, stamped boldly in the
rectangle in the top right-hand corner.

"Christ," she said, jiggling the receiver stand and
dialling again. He crossed the room and pretended to
be interested in the life of Horseman's Yard. The maid
was gossiping with the postman now, both green faces
creased into laughter, both sets of teeth yellow and
gapped.

"Extension thirty-six," said the girl. "Hello, Sue, this
is Kate. How's the car going? ... Great. Can I speak to
Mussolini? No, it's important. Thanks ... Hi, Dad ...
Yes, sorry, but you've got to sort this out—there's a
fellow turned up here called ... damn, I've forgotten..."

"Humayan."

"That's right, he's called Humayan, and he says he's
the fellow who's going to have Moirag's room ... yes, of
course ... he's got a letter from you, all about rent and
things ... Oh, but Christ, Dad, of course he's the right
fellow, but he's (look, I'm sorry, Mr. Thing) he's brown
... more coffee than milk ... no, of course I think it's
all right, but what about *Mum*? ... She's at the dentist
with Glenda, you know that, you changed the appointment ... yes, his Card's OK, he showed me, it says Saxon
... But *Mum*! ... No, I bloody well won't—it's nothing
to do with *me*. You've bloody well got to sort it out. OK,
listen, I'll get him out of the house and keep him happy
for an hour—I'll put his bag in my room ... but you
can bloody well come home and sort it out with Mum
... It's nothing to do with *me* ... OK, so long. Christ."

She spoke the last word to herself as she put the telephone down with a bang.

"Some misunderstanding?" said Humayan gently. He had often told himself on the journey that he was bound to meet occasional patches of prejudice during his stay in England and that he would school himself to ignore them. Now he saw that the schooling would be harder than he had expected.

"The bloody twit," said the girl. "The bloody arrogant twit. Look, Mr. ... look, we've got to clear out before Mum comes home. Dad's coming back to sort it out with her. You go out of the Yard, turn left at the lights and wait for me at the next lights. I'll be about ten minutes. The Zone ends there, so we can go around together. OK?"

In fact he had to wait almost quarter of an hour at the lights, but occupied the time pleasantly enough, watching the passers-by and thinking about the girl. She was several inches taller than he was, but that would be true of almost any Englishwoman he met, and in this case he found the notion stimulating. He wondered whether she too ... at least she had refused to let him carry his case up to her bedroom; perhaps that was a natural first reaction to a feeling of sexual attraction. The whole situation was very promising. He did not feel at all alarmed by the momentary difficulty over Mrs. Glister's reception of him, because he was confident in the knowledge of favourable planets.

His eye was caught by a brilliant blob of mauve on the other side of the road, a large and glossy pram pushed by a weary young green woman. Clear through the traffic Humayan could hear the squall of infant lungs. The mother stopped, balanced a paper carrier-bag on the foot of the pram and took from it two bottles; she used the bag to screen what she was doing from the crowds on her side of the street; rapidly she eased the teat off the baby's bottle and poured into the orange-juice a shot of brandy from the other bottle; then with a quick glance over her shoulder she herself took a swig at the brandy-bottle and thrust it back into the carrier-bag before

13

giving the baby its own bottle. The squalling ceased.

"Bloody nit," said a voice at Humayan's shoulder. "She'll get picked up."

Miss Glister had changed, not merely her clothes but her appearance. She was dressed now in a coarse, peasant-looking smock and her pink skin was smeared with a make-up which hinted vaguely at olive. The lights were now against them, so they stood and waited.

"How does one distinguish the border of a Zone?" said Humayan.

"You don't," she said. "You're supposed to know. But when you've been here a couple of weeks you'll find you can smell it. Get to a Green Zone, though, and you'll see the riot barriers stacked up. You're not allowed in there. Right, let's cross."

She took his arm and nannied him over the road, but let go as soon as they were on the far pavement.

"I have read about the zoning laws," he said stiffly. "I was not aware that persons of different races were forbidden to walk together in a Saxon Zone."

"They aren't *forbidden*, but good as because the pigs don't like it. Specially if you're young. They take you in and question you, a couple of days sometimes, and then let you go. It happened to a girl I know and she's had the twitch ever since. So it's not worth the risk. But it's OK in a mixed zone like this. What does P stand for?"

"I regret . . ."

"You said your name was P. P. Thing. What does P stand for?"

"Ah. I see. The first P stands for Pravandragasharatipili. The second P does not stand for anything. I chose it for euphony."

"Christ! D'you mind . . . well . . . I mean . . . is it OK if I call you Pete?"

"That will be quite acceptable."

"Great. I'm Kate, unless Mum's in earshot."

Well, this was progress, thought Humayan. Pete Humayan. A definite step towards intimacy. He tried to match his pace to hers as she wound her way down the

14

crowded pavement. This was a quite different area from the one in which the Glisters lived; the brass dolphin door-knockers were gone, and the glistening paint, and the kempt window-boxes. This was all shops, every second one of which seemed to sell either shoes or refrigerators. The shops were clean, neon-lit and spacious, but the pavements were busy and dirty. For the first time Humayan saw green citizens not working at necessary jobs such as carrying travellers' luggage or cleaning windows, but moving and frowning as though they had lives and problems of their own. He saw several policemen, of both colours, all armed.

"This way," said Kate and swung through an inadequate gap in the traffic, so that Humayan had to scutter for the central island. On the north side of the road ornate red-brick buildings showed raddled above the glistening shop-fronts, but on the south these had been completely pulled down and a whole new shopping precinct erected round a central tower of offices. Kate led him out of the fretting traffic into a patio for pedestrians where leaves and sweet-wrappers swirled in little fey tornadoes generated by the micro-climate of the tower. It seemed inconceivable that anybody should ever want to sit here, but there were benches in the middle of the patio, rather like those one finds in large old-fashioned art-galleries, which enable the high-souled visitor to rest while he studies classic rapes and martyrdoms. So here it seemed that the benches had been provided for the really enthusiastic shopper to sit for an hour and feast his eyes and soul on the façade of the Olde Chick'n'burger Eaterie or the Cutique. Not a soul was so doing.

But when the patio turned the corner to round the back of the tower every bench was full.

"Hey! They must be good!" said Kate. "We'll have to sit on the ground."

In the middle of the paved waste, between the benches, rose cylindrical columns lit from within so that the advertisements they carried glowed with factitious warmth. Kate immediately settled cross-legged with her back to one of these. Humayan was shocked. It was four years since he had last sat on a pavement, and then it had been considerably warmer than this one looked; but by good fortune there was a litter-bin handy into which someone had dropped a clean-looking newspaper. He folded it smooth and settled with dignity on to a head-line that screamed to his unheeding buttocks 'ENVOY SNATCHED!'

When he was settled he noticed the noise. After a few seconds' bafflement he decided that it might be music. Yes. Outside one of the shops, a purveyor of electric equipment called The Shamrock, a group of young men sat with their instruments. Two of them were genuinely green, and the other four, though patently Saxon, made gestures in the direction of greenness; they had dyed their hair carrots and wore suits of baggy sacking. The girls nearest them wore the same sort of green-tinged make-up as Kate, and smocks, and head scarfs knotted under their chins. Two of the musicians were playing small harps wired to amplifiers provided by the shop. One young man was singing a song whose long notes seemed to emerge through his nose and after being processed by the microphone and speakers to bounce with a plaintive twang off the shop façades.

"My wild colonial baaaaaaaaabe," he sang.

"Irish, with Welsh backing," said Kate. "They're a bit of a phoney, these mixed groups, but he can sing and that lead harpist is brilliant."

"You would like to listen, or you would like to talk?" said Humayan.

"Talk," she said. "You see, Pete ... well ... I mean ..."

She frowned. He realised that she was embarrassed, and irritated with him because of her embarrassment. He did not consider this a very promising mood for increasing her interest in him, and decided that a definite manly openness would be the most suitable attitude.

"I will explain my own position," he said. "I am a medical statistician ..."

"Christ! How did that happen?"

"Oh, quite simply. My father had a very good horoscope drawn when I was born. He paid a lot of money, believe me. The astrologer said that I was destined to be a healer, so my father proposed to educate me in medicine. But horoscopes do not tell everything, and my one did not say that I was a genius."

She laughed.

"Oh, it is quite true. I promise you. A teacher, a missionary from Aberdeen, discovered this fact when I was three. I am a mathematical genius. It is not common, but it occurs. In some ways it is like having a very rare disease. You can look up the other cases in books. It was more astonishing when I was three, of course. But I can still tell you the cube of any five-figure number you mention, in two or three seconds, and remember any number I have ever seen. Would you like me to demonstrate?"

"Christ, no!"

He was disappointed but not abashed. No beautiful seducible woman he had ever met had been remotely impressed by his one supreme gift. Only he had hoped it might be different in England.

"Oh, I am not a creative mathematician," he said. "Not Boole, not Godel. I just breathe numbers. Other people have had this gift, this knack, and often it has made them most unhappy because they could not use it. But now, in a world where we have modern computers, it is a great convenience. I can do things with a computer which are not just mathematical tricks. I could show you ... no, you are not interested."

"Yes I am, Pete. Honestly. Please go on."

"No. I will tell you what happened to me and why I am in England. My father, who was a wise man, looked around India and saw how many people were dying. He said to me, 'Pravi, you cannot heal them all. It is a waste of your gift to heal only a few. You must use your gift in the field of healing.' So I became a medical statistician. I had passed all my exams with top honours. That is not boasting, it is true. So I could choose among jobs, almost anything I wanted. My father was dead now, so I made enquiries and found there is more money in cancer research than any other field. Even in poor India there is lots of money in cancer research, because that is what the rich men are afraid of. So I set to work to build up a reputation in that field. You understand?"

17

Her nod was only slightly bored, only slightly baffled.

"Good. Now came my fate. I decided to work on the hereditary factors in liability to cancer, because the data is there but has never been properly analysed. I had the use of a little old computer at my university, so to make the most of it I had to arrange my material in particular ways. Nobody else could have done this. Now, one large set of figures had been gathered in Britain, and included all the relevant hereditary material, including racial origins. And of course skin colour—this is because there are some forms of skin cancer which are related to the reaction of the skin to ultra-violet radiation, and that in turn is related to the production of melanin and chloronin by the skin. All right?"

She was thoroughly bored now. Or was she? Perhaps, he thought, this was a normal reaction—a sort of putting-out-of-the-mind—in this society to any subject which seemed to relate uncomfortably to its central and basic problem. He didn't care. He was going to surprise her now.

"It was all very dull," he said. "I shuffled my figures about and found nothing. I shuffled them again and found nothing. But all the time, in that jungle of columns, my fate was waiting like a tiger. I shuffled again and the tiger sprang. I solved the mystery of the Green Gene."

"You did what?"

"I perceived a relationship between a number of genetic factors and the point at which a population group of a given size, among whom the chloronin-forming gene is present but dormant, suddenly produces a preponderance of green babies. This has always been a mystery. Now it is a mystery no more, thanks to me."

"But that's brilliant!"

"Oh, I do not say that. It was fate. I had arranged my figures for a quite different purpose, but I had my shape of mind and perceived this correlation in the arrangement. It stuck out like a..."

"Sore thumb?"

"No no no. Like the dome of a temple in the plains."

"Well, what's the answer?"

18

"Oh, I cannot explain that to you. It is very technical."

"Try."

The attempt was a failure but not a disaster. He could see that she was now deeply impressed.

"It does not matter," he said at last. "And there is much work still to be done. I have merely made a beginning. So there I was, Miss Kate—my fate had sprung from the jungle and pinned me down. At first I thought it a simple dilemma—I had stumbled on an interesting but useless piece of knowledge. There was no money in it, but there might be prestige, and in the end prestige is money too. Ought I to forsake the certain gains of cancer research for the possible gains of genetic research? It was a moral question."

He paused to emphasise the spiritual drama, the wrestling in a man's soul in far Bombay.

"But that's fascinating!" she said. "You mean you can tell whether I'm going to have a green baby—I mean supposing I were going to have a baby at all?"

"Well, not precisely," said Humayan, allowing even in the lack of precision for still wider margins of error. "There are all kinds..."

"I must tell Francis."

"Who is she? Is she about to give birth?" said Humayan, with all the male Indian's fastidious shrinking from anything to do with midwifery. Kate laughed.

"He's our neighbour in the Yard. His name's as bad as yours to spell, P-R-A-O-N-S-A-I-S, I think. Francis Leary, but he calls himself Frank Lear for professional purposes. He's a journalist specialising in the Green Question."

"Oh yes?" said Humayan, implying the negative. "Well, I had better cut my long story short. I went to my Director and told him what I had found, and he also was part of my fate, for in his youth he had played cricket for a team captained by the Maharaja of Bhurtpore, and one of his team-mates is now a senior official in your Race Relations Board. So there was no escape. They offered me a very good salary to continue my genetic research here in London. Here I am."

"You've come to work for the RRB?" she said.

"Yes."

"Oh."

She looked away. Humayan sensed this sudden withdrawal of confidence, but didn't understand it. He watched two young green men performing a complicated form of jig to the music of the harpists. They were beginning to whoop between leaps when a couple of policemen strolled round the corner of the patio and rapped them perfunctorily on the skulls with their truncheons. The jiggers subsided. The owner of the shop, a stout, bald man, came out and spoke briefly with the policemen, who turned away and walked on. These policemen were green, and their faces seamed and hard. Humayan saw their four pale eyes flick to where he sat and stay fixed. The brows frowned and the strides faltered, but then the shoulders shrugged and they passed on. He watched the scurrying shoppers move instinctively clear of their path until they rounded the next corner.

"Yes, I'm paid by the RRB," he said, swallowing unnecessary spittle. "But my work will be entirely objective, neutral. I am simply going to find out the truth."

"Why did you come to us?" she said, still not looking at him.

"I advertised for accommodation in a magazine, and your father wrote to me."

"The magazine was called *Prism*?" she said.

"Yes. It is an impressive publication."

"It had bloody well better be," she said. "Dad's the editor."

"I don't understand," he said. "My Director in Bombay showed me this paper and suggested that I . . ."

"*Prism* is a glossy magazine devoted to racial problems. I've never met anybody who buys it—any person I mean. Institutions subscribe to it and leave it on tables in their reception areas, but even so it loses a packet of money. It's kept going by a front organisation called the Council for Citizenship, and I've never heard of anybody who belongs to that either. The Council gets its money from a few big firms—Francis knows their names—which want to keep things as they are—cheap green labour and all that—but don't mind spending a bit on a pseud paper

20

which makes people—you know, people like the Americans and your Director and so on—think it's all not so bad as all that and we're doing the best we can. Did you read it?"

Humayan nodded, shocked. Most of his knowledge of Britain had come from the three copies of *Prism* which the Director had lent him. He had considered it a very reliable organ.

"You're the first I've ever met, not counting Dad. And I'm not sure *he* does. Did you see any pictures in it of Greens who weren't smiling?"

"I do not remember."

"Well, I can tell you you didn't. Greens smile in *Prism*, just like names of books go into italic. It's a real pseud, and Dad's main worry is not what he puts into it but how he persuades the backers that anybody in the wide world reads it; he's hit on a cunning wheeze, which is to print pages and pages of small ads from all over the world. He writes them all himself, because he can't trust any of his staff not to slip in a joke one. And then, out of the blue, you send him a genuine ad. What does he do?"

"He prints it?"

"He *answers* it, nut-head ... Pete, I mean."

"Why?"

"Well, that's Dad. He's got this idea he's an honest man—*the* honest man. Mum's been at him to let Moirag's room before I install some shaggy boy-friend, so a far-flung scientist was a godsend, but that was a side-issue. *Prism* pays his salary, so he has to feel sure it's doing a useful, worthwhile job, never mind how much he fakes it up. But it gives his conscience a few twinges, so he reacts by acting double-honourable anywhere it doesn't matter, like your ad. Anyone else would have chucked it away, but he made sure you got at least one answer—and then he didn't have the nerve to tell Mum quite what he'd done, bringing in a ... a ..."

"Brown," he said.

"Young," she said.

"Foreign," he said.

"Genius," she said.

"Bombabomba bombabomba bombabomba bombabomba bomb!" sang the young man, beginning the syllables without a meaning and finishing with one.

"They got something this morning, just before you came," said Kate. "I heard the windows rattle."

Humayan remembered the shuffling of air that had diverted the policemen outside McWatter's Auld Bothie. He decided that the explosion had been remote enough to be brave about.

"I do not at all wish to distress your mother," he lied.

"Doesn't matter. Dad will get his own way. He does it on purpose, sort of, pushing her as far as she'll go, and seeing her come to heel again. He does it for kicks. Glenda—she's my kid sister, sixteen, quite like him in some ways—she's got him taped. She says he thinks he's God, only he's too bloody lazy to do any godding. He'll get his way with Mum, puffing at his pipe and stroking the back of his neck and talking in that soft voice as though he's the only reasonable person in the whole bloody world—oh Christ, he makes me vomit. He's always showing his right-mindedness with symbols. You're one— a nice safe symbol of liberal attitudes which won't get him into any trouble with anyone. But he never lifts a finger to do anything which will make the slightest difference to the whole bloody situation. He sits there at *Prism* drawing his salary and persuading himself that if he doesn't print another six pictures of smiling Greens the world will be a bloody sight worse off than it is already."

Humayan considered Doctor Glister's attitude to be a very proper and responsible one for the father of a family, but chose not to say so. Kate was slightly flushed with her anger, and her pretty bosom seemed to have grown more emphatic under the loose orange smock. These were hopeful auguries. Her emotion might well be sexual, but for sound psychological reasons she was diverting it into anger against her father. He ran a judicious index finger down the line of his moustache.

"I do not wish to be an embarrassment to anybody," he said. "What will your mother really feel?"

"Oh, Mum's all right. She's dead honest, once you've

22

learnt her language. And anyway nothing that happens outside her own family is really real to her nowadays. Once she's decided you're clean and quiet and won't spoil our chances of marrying a couple of chartered accountants, she'll start telling the neighbours what a jewel you are. It's all her idea, really. The new zoning laws came in this year and Moirag had to move out, though she still comes in daily, so Mum started to worry about the empty room. That's the sort of thing she worries about, not bombs and kidnappings. Her excuse is that she wants to build up capital so that when we're married she can retire to Hertfordshire and breed her horrible little dogs."

"I see," said Humayan, carefully registering that he must not allow it to become apparent to Mrs. Glister that he was any impediment to Kate's reception as a virgin bride into the bed of some young lion of finance.

"By the way," said Kate, "I know it sounds awful to say it, but you've got to watch Moirag. She rips off."

"She is an exhibitionist?"

"Bad luck. Anyway she's hideous. No, I mean she takes things—anything she can sell for brandy. She's morally justified of course, but it's a nuisance. You just have to watch her."

"I see. Thank you for telling me. And your sister?"

"Glenda? You've got to watch her too."

"About, er, ripping off?"

"About everything."

"All is changed utterly," sang the singer.

"Yeah, feller, yeah," agreed the rest of the group.

"A terrible beauty is booooooooooooorn," sang the singer.

The group agreed with him again.

"I think I've gone off him," said Kate. "Pity you weren't here yesterday. There was a chap with the electric bagpipes—he was *brilliant*."

II

MR. MARVLE (Exeter) *asked the Minister for Education what progress was being made in the replacement in State Secondary Schools of out-of-date history textbooks, especially those dealing with Celtic affairs.*

LADY PYNE (Hove Central): *The withdrawal of erroneous textbooks, begun under the Butler administration, was scandalously allowed to lapse under the Socialist Government. But since last year I have been giving this matter top priority and the process is almost complete. It is better for children not to be taught at all than for them to be taught wrong.* (Government cheers.)

MR. MARVLE: *So far so good. But what about the introduction of new textbooks based on the latest historical research?*

LADY PYNE: *This is a more difficult matter. Research is proceeding under the auspices of the Race Relations Board. But I am sorry to have to tell the House that many scholars have refused to abandon the myths—often patently absurd and even wicked myths—on which their reputation is founded. It has been a matter of discovering historians and scientists of real calibre who are prepared to take a more realistic view of the social function of history.*

Doctor Glister was not a large man, but he managed to move and hold himself as though he was. Indeed, though he was not actually fat either, he looked as though he could be the moment he chose, like one of those fish that is able to puff itself to a threatening size at the approach of danger. He wore heavy spectacles, had a bald but freckled dome and a trim grey beard. His eyes were mild and brown and slightly bloodshot. A curving pipe projected from moist lips.

"Come in, come in," he said. "Kate, you'd better get out of that rig before your mother sees you."

His voice was almost a whisper, which Humayan later discovered was normal to him, but there in the hall it sounded like complicity with his daughter against the great matriarchal plot. Kate ran up the stairs.

"Come in, come in," said Doctor Glister again, holding open the door into the living room so that there was no hand for Humayan to shake. "Mrs. Glister is a little distressed at the moment, I'm sorry to say."

"About my arrival?"

"No no, my dear fellow. We are both delighted about that. No, no. I don't know whether you heard an explosion this morning. It turns out they got Harrods."

"The knitwear department," said a new voice, rough with sorrow.

Mrs. Glister was sitting on the longest, lowest sofa. She was skinny and blonde, and was mopping from a cold blue eye the last spillage of her emotion.

"It'll all be in the papers tomorrow," she said.

"I think not, Mother," said Doctor Glister. "This is Mr. Humayan."

The words were a call from the tents of grief to the ramparts of duty. She rose from the sofa and inspected Humayan with her head tilted slightly to one side, as though at that angle her sharply defined nose obstructed her vision less.

"Well," she said, as she settled back after letting him feel the chill touch of three bony fingers, "I hear that you are coming to stay with us for a few weeks."

"Months, Mother," said Doctor Glister. The whisper made his remark sound wholly emotionless.

"No doubt it will all sort itself out," said Mrs. Glister.

Had it not been for Kate, now decelticising herself upstairs—perhaps at this very moment deliciously naked

25

—Humayan would have offered to leave. As it was he tried to imitate Doctor Glister and speak without anger.

"I would be honoured to reside here," he said. "I do not wish to be a nuisance or embarrassment to anybody. I am clean and quiet and tidy, I think."

He thought he detected a slight softening of Mrs. Glister's face, and at the same time a hardening of her glance, as though she appreciated his sentiments but did not quite believe them. She reminded him uncomfortably of his grandmother. As she started to speak again the door opened behind him and the two dogs came yelping in, scampered on to the sofa and wrestled for places on Mrs. Glister's exiguous lap, where they turned to stare bulbous-eyed at the intruder.

"I've fed the little rats," said the girl who came behind them. "Who's this?"

She was dark and spectacled and rather plain, but not with the plainness of a girl who has grown to a woman's size without yet feeling ready for a woman's role; the bones of her face were strong, and she had her mother's nose; but for her maroon school uniform her age would have been unguessable. Perhaps she knew that she would never look succulent, and so was training to become an aunt. She stared at Humayan with knowing aggressiveness.

"Hello," she said, "I'm Glenda."

"Anne," protested Mrs. Glister.

"Mum's slid a bit to the right since she christened us," said the girl.

"My name is Humayan. Er, Pete Humayan."

"I bet it's not."

"Anne!"

"You are right, miss. My real name is very long and difficult."

"And anyone who knows it has power over you."

Humayan shook his head, startled. His horoscope had told that he would travel far and be troubled with a witch, but had not linked the two prophecies. Was it possible that here, in this brusque and unmagical room, he had met her? She had a witch's eyes behind those spectacles.

"I am not superstitious," he said bravely.

Doctor Glister had been listening with an amused look while he applied successive matches to his pipe.

"Let's call him Pete," he said.

"I think the children should call him Mr. Humayan," said Mrs. Glister. "I certainly shall. I was not expecting a crowd for luncheon, Mr. Humayan, so I've got no food in the house. But if you'd like to come to supper this first evening, so that we can get to know each other . . ."

"I should be most honoured."

"Will you show him Moirag's old room, Anne?"

"You've got your own kitchen and bath, see? That's the old zoning laws, before this new lot. Greens in domestic service had to be separately accommodated, which meant having their own plumbing and cooking, in London anyway. I bet Moirag never had a shower, and she nicked all her food out of our kitchen . . ."

Humayan sat on the edge of the bed and watched Glenda with growing alarm as she banged drawers open and shut and flung the cupboard door wide. She actually disappeared right into the cupboard, then came out grinning and threw herself down by the bed and peered under it.

"Checking for empty bottles," she said. "Moirag's half-drunk in the mornings and fully drunk in the evenings —they all are. Luckily she's got a head like iron, but she does hide her empties in funny places. They aren't allowed to drink anything stronger than beer, har har. I expect you don't drink at all, being a whatever you are."

"I have no religion, but I do not drink."

"Dad's a humanist. Very wet."

"His humanism permits him to drink to excess?"

"What? Oh, *wet*. No, I meant creepy, boring, yuck. That's what humanism is, religionwise. I'm a latter-day Satanist, though I still have to attend school prayers. I sing the hymns backwards. They only make us go to prayers to be counted. That's what education is, being counted once a day at prayers and once a year at exams."

"Counting people is very important. I do it for a living."

"Is it? Well, let me tell you we latter-day Satanists worship the great Minus One, because when everybody's been killed there's going to be one more death than there was life, which will make the great Minus One plus, and he'll rule the universe."

"That is very philosophical."

"Is it?"

She knelt up, sounding pleased for the first time.

"I think so. And did you know that minus one possesses two imaginary cube roots, other than minus one itself, and each is the square of the other to all eternity?"

"No! That's great! I'll tell Helen and we'll work it into our prayer-book. She's the other latter-day Satanist, and *she* has to go to church in the holidays. She's got a really yuck family, even worse than mine. Show me how this cube-root thing works."

She sat beside him on the bed while he did the equation on the back of an envelope. She got it at once.

"I suppose it would work just as well for plus one."

"Yes."

"That's a pity ... still ... Why have you come here?"

"I have been hired to try and explain and forecast the growth in the number of green children born to parents with white skins but mixed racial origins."

"I didn't know the number was growing."

"But in your history books..."

"They won't teach us any British History. It's all foul Japanese."

"Oh, well. The facts are simple, but the explanation is extremely complicated. Your so-called Celts are in fact a people of very mixed racial origins, as are your so-called Saxons. Until the fourteenth century the occurrence of the green gene as a dominant was rare enough to escape mention, but then in Ireland, Scotland and Wales there was a sudden surge in the number of green births, enough to make up five per cent of the population —though that is guessing, of course. The records are very bad. The numbers stayed like that for several generations, and then there was another surge, and another in the

28

last century, though that was disguised by the enormous growth in population of all colours. Nobody knew what caused these surges, but I happened to be doing some work on something else and stumbled across the beginnings of an explanation, so here I am."

"But why us?"

He explained briefly about the advertisement in *Prism*, and Kate's interpretation.

Still kneeling Glenda took off her spectacles and stared at him. Without the screening glass he could see that she had a strong cast in her left eye. Her gaze made him feel very uncomfortable, as though she already knew all there was to be known about him, and there was as little point in trying to hide from her search as there is from the snuffling monster in a nightmare. She shook her head when he'd finished.

"Kate's got a very simple view of Dad. He must have some reason for mucking Mum about. Dad is always..."

She stopped, cocked her head to listen and put her glasses back on. Humayan heard a faint scrabbling at the door. One of the dogs, he thought.

"Come in," shouted Glenda.

Doctor Glister's bearded head poked round the door as though there was no neck or body behind it.

"Ah, there you are, Glenny," he said, and came creeping into the room. "I'll drop you at school on my way back to the office. All well, Pete? I trust you don't think I've misled you in our correspondence."

"On the contrary. You have been exceedingly veracious."

Doctor Glister blinked and smiled.

"Veracity is one of my weak points," he said. "I ought to take lessons in lying from Glenny. Well, I'll see you this evening then."

He crept away.

"You're in luck," said Glenda. "It's Moirag's evening off, so Mum will be cooking. She's good. See you."

As soon as she was gone Humayan locked the door and removed the key.

The architect who had designed Horseman's Yard had

29

needed a ruthless ingenuity to comply with the old zoning laws without wasting on greens any space a white might fancy. The separate cell for a domestic servant was fitted into the interstices of other, better-proportioned rooms. No one much larger than Humayan would have been able to use the shower at all. No one had, anyway. A buttress-like projection in the lavatory wall forced the occupant to rest most of his weight on his left buttock; rumours in the buttress told Humayan it was a water-tank. The bedroom too was niched and nooked wherever the amenities of a neighbouring room had been given priority. There was an exiguous hanging cupboard, and the furniture was the bed, one upright chair, and a chest all of whose drawers stuck in different fashions and needed different knacks to open or shut them.

Humayan unpacked slowly, choosing the best possible location for every item and making a fastidious bundle of the dirty laundry of his voyage. He discovered in the process that the room was far from clean, with dust and scraps in any corner that could not immediately be reached by a perfunctory sweeper; none of these fragments told him anything about the previous occupant, except that she used bright brass hairpins, but after a while the knowledge of her became oppressive in the tiny space, a life lived under these conditions, squeezed into the crannies left between the Glisters' lives, full of hard angles and restrictions, and now swept away by a force as impersonal to her and blind as famine or a tidal wave. He began to think he could smell the slightly sour sweat of a middle-aged unwashing woman, mixed with the taint of brandy dregs. He opened the window.

The bright noon was full of a single voice, as monotonous as a heartbeat, as harsh as the cry of a peacock.

"One-ah! Two-ah! Three-ah! Foooouuuurr! One-ah! Two-ah! Three-ah! Fooooouuuurr!"

It came from beyond the yellow wall which provided the whole view from his window. He leaned out and saw that the same featureless blank ran the whole length of this side of Horseman's Yard; at its foot each house

30

in the Yard had its own area of dustbins and other un-
sightlinesses, segregated here so that the central courtyard should remain spruce and jolly. He also saw that the
architect had chosen to enliven this façade with a single
unifying detail, a ledge that ran all along the Yard about
two feet below the windows, a highway for burglars. It
was a bally nuisance, he thought. He would have to
lock his window whenever he went out. Being a cautious
man, he would have locked his window in any case, but
still it was a nuisance to have to. A bally nuisance.

When he had unpacked he took his dirty clothes to a
laundromat, and while they were washing found an un-
vandalised phone-booth and rang the Race Relations
Board, to make sure that he would be expected when he
arrived for his new job next morning. He ate a flavourless omelette at a restaurant, then strolled round the
zone, admiring the tree-lined streets and the flower-packed
gardens and the commanding voices of pink children
calling to their green nursemaids. When he was tired of
that he went back to Horseman's Yard and lay on his
bed, considering possible next steps on the road to becoming Kate's lover. He decided to buy a book on sitar-
music, and pretend to know something of that art. All
music is mathematics, after all.

Mrs. Glister could indeed cook. Somehow the consciousness of a beautiful meal made the period after supper
quite bearable, when it should have been an agony. The
five of them sat round in the living room and constructed
conversations, awkward little edifices of ill-mortared remarks, not combining into any coherent street or village.
Mrs. Glister seemed able to converse only about people
she knew; ideas and generalisations were intolerably
foreign to her, nor would she permit anything that bore
in any way on the racial situation. Even so, she did most
of the Glisters' talking, for the Doctor himself seemed to
relish most the intervals in the conversation, filling them
with bubbling sucks at his extinct pipe. Kate lay on the
floor on her stomach in a pose that stretched her
trousers tight round the hummock of her buttocks,
leafing through magazines that she had evidently read

31

before. Glenda played patience but glanced up from time to time to demolish any conversation that seemed likely to grow into a meaningful shape; Humayan came to the conclusion that she was not only dangerous but unappealing, a jolly awkward customer, in fact. He welcomed the television news as a merciful relaxation, but when it was over Mrs. Glister said with a sigh that was almost a sob, "Nothing about Harrods."

Doctor Glister grunted with a faint note of warning —perhaps it was that that made Glenda join in.

"What about Harrods?" she said.

"They blew it up. The knitwear department. That nice Mavis is dead and Mrs. Grant has lost an arm. Only we're not supposed to know. Animals!"

"Have you studied our dogs, Pete?" said Doctor Glister.

"Yes, indeed, sir. I have not seen dogs of this type before. Are they, er ..."

Mrs. Glister smiled and turned one of the animals over to tickle its flabby, pinkish belly; but it responded with an erection of its minuscule instrument, so she cuffed it to the floor and turned her attention to the other one.

"Yes, they're very rare," she said. "They're called Boogers. It's quite an interesting story. Show Mr. Humayan the picture, Anne."

With an indecipherable mutter Glenda got off the floor and fetched a photographic album, which she flipped through and plonked open on Humayan's lap. The picture was a reproduction of a painting, showing an interior in which a number of red-faced rustics were playing a card-game. A dog exactly like the one in Mrs. Glister's lap was pissing against the table-leg. At the bottom were the words 'Adrian van Bugger. Dutch School'.

"That's a very famous painting," said Mrs. Glister, "and Booger was an artist who always drew every detail accurately. Look at those pans above the stove. But the dog was quite different from any known breed until my cousin retired from the army and decided to try and breed a dog exactly like the one in the picture. You see, that way he'd get a much *purer* strain of dog than almost all the known breeds, which are only Victorian develop-

32

ments, or even later. But we know from the picture that Boogers existed three hundred years ago. Only we're having a dreadful fight with the Kennel Club to get the breed recognised."

"I'm sorry," said Humayan. His Director at the University had told him what useful words these were in England.

"Yes," sighed Mrs. Glister, "the Kennel Club's so stuffy, you see, and they won't recognise a breed until it's bred true for several generations. The trouble is that when you get Boogers looking right, like the one in the picture, they don't breed any more. They're quite nice little dogs, but they just aren't interested in breeding. My cousin uses artificial insemination, and then the bitches make terrible mothers and he has to hand-rear the pups. It's such a pity. I'm sure there'll be a lot of money in them if we can only sort out their emotional problems. When the girls are grown up I'm..."

"The truth is," said Glenda, "that van Bugger was the hell of a painter of doorways and three-legged stools and dead rabbits, but he couldn't paint anything alive. Not for nuts. Look at those men—you've never seen men like that, have you? The same with the dog. He painted it all wrong. There never was a dog that shape, so naturally when you breed one that shape the others don't recognise it's a dog at all, and don't see any point in having sex with it. They'll go yelping after any bitch that really looks like a dog. Mrs. Smith-Higgins's collie..."

"It's worse than that," said Kate, stretching with luxuriant boredom. "He dropped a dog-shaped blob of paint on the canvas and was too lazy to clean it off, so he just added a leg or two and a widdle. Cousin Ranulph's spent his retirement trying to breed a blob."

"It is an interesting genetic experiment," said Humayan. "What are their names?"

"They are called Want and Ought," said Doctor Glister.

"Oh, that is very philosophical," said Humayan. "Which is which?"

"I have not made up my mind."

"They are a new acquisition?"

"Far from it. We've had them for three years, haven't we, my dear. The enigma of desire and duty . . ."

"And that's not philosophical, that's plain bloody laziness," said Kate, with the same lovely rage that the police state had evoked in her that morning. Doctor Glister looked pleased and Mrs. Glister sat stiff on the sofa and smiled the dead smile of a mother who has heard all her children's favourite jokes many, many times.

Eventually that day, Tuesday, ended.

Planetary favour was still beaming down on Humayan when he returned from his first day's work. Even the jostles and stares of the commuter-packed Saxons-only compartment of the tube had done nothing to weigh down his buoyancy. His office was for himself alone, newly equipped, and containing a computer input console more sophisticated than any he had ever used. The Director had invited him to take coffee in his office— that had been particularly gratifying, for the Director was a most impressive figure—at least a most impressive figurehead, gaunt and tall with curling great eyebrows over deep-set eyes. He had made a perfectly delightful speech of welcome, about the honour Humayan was doing the RRB by coming so far to help them with their difficult and vital task, and then he had talked with fervour and knowledge about varieties of Indian cooking, until Humayan's mouth watered with memories. The interview had lasted so long that when Humayan left he found two impatient-looking gentlemen waiting in the office of the Director's secretary.

And then his new colleagues in the section of the RRB known as the Laboratory had been equally friendly, and even a touch effusive. At first Humayan had thought that this was in recognition of his own calibre and achievements; but later he decided that it was a subconscious attempt to demonstrate that here, in the hub and power-house of racial research, men were scientists, free from any but objective considerations of a brown skin. He thought this a proper attitude. He was a scientist too, a counter of people.

34

A new voice was muttering in the Glisters' kitchen. He slid past and up the stairs, and found a note pinned to his door: "Sir, Please do not lock your door, or how can I be cleaning your room? Moirag McBain." The writing sloped far to the right; the author had had two goes at spelling the word 'cleaning'.

Humayan took out a pencil from the array in his breast-pocket and wrote, "Thank you, but I will clean the room myself. PH." He unlocked the door and went in. He had brought home a fattish cyclostyled folder which contained the rules and vocabulary of the big RRB computer, which he would henceforth be using; at a glance he had seen that it was an ingenious but quite complex extension of Algol; it was classified 'Secret' and no doubt they had expected him to keep it in his office and refer to it as he used his console; but he preferred to learn the whole thing off in one go, partly because this would simplify his work, but mainly because he knew it would enormously impress his new colleagues to find him on wholly familiar terms with the big machine next morning. He thought it would take him about five hours, provided he wasn't interrupted.

Almost at once he heard the faint scratching that seemed to mean Doctor Glister was at the door.

"Come in," he called.

There was no answer, but the scratching continued, so he rose and opened the door to find Glenda poised on the landing with a pencil in her hand, looking not at all startled to find her writing surface suddenly removed from her. She had been adding graffiti to Moirag's note: MAKE DIRT, NOT LOVE; BAN THE BRUSH; HOOVER MUST GO. Her imitation of Humayan's script was quite good.

"You will get me into trouble with the servants," he said angrily.

She grinned at him. Her eyes behind the lenses were sharp with malice. He snatched the note from the door and took it back into his room, where he rubbed out all her additions. It was some time before he could settle to the computer language again.

*   *   *

35

He was hanging up his suit, his mind content as a snake in the sun after its big feed of figures, when he noticed a little beam of light from the back of the tiny cupboard; he had already worked out that the architect had designed one cupboard-space here, between his room and the next, most of which served the other side, leaving only this chimney-like space for his own clothes. Occasionally during his study a wash of music had seeped through the wall, but he had been too deep in concentration to consider it. Now a faint memory of busy drums and wailing voices told him whose room might lie beyond the chink. It was too high for his line of sight, so he very quietly removed his suits and placed a small pile of *Statistical Journals* on the floor of the cupboard. They gave him the necessary stature.

Kate was in bed, lying on her stomach, reading a book; an eiderdown concealed her shape and when she reached out an arm to look at her bedside clock he saw that she wore banal striped pyjamas.

He woke early, and told himself that there was no point in lying in bed, so he dressed and shaved and crept into the cupboard. She was still asleep; it appeared that she liked to sleep with an open window, for the draught through the spyhole was thin and agonising. After five minutes his right eye was weeping uncontrollably, so he turned his head away and listened for the first sound of movement. To pass the time he ran unnecessarily through the computer language he had learnt the night before. It was all there, of course, stored as neatly and accessibly as any information in the big machine itself. Each time he forced his eye into the sword-like draught he found Kate still sleeping; but when at last she woke she yawned, looked at her clock, flung back the blankets, staggered to the window, closed the catch and washed and dressed out of sight. It was infuriating: and odd, too, that whoever had made the spyhole—and it was clearly more than an accident—had thought it worth while if that was the sum of the performance.

His eye wept all day, so that he had to close it and use only the left eye to consider the results output from his console. On the other hand his colleagues were properly astounded at his mastery of their difficult language. He began to contemplate a few minor sophistications that would help him with his work; and also to investigate as far as he could the nature and coding of the supervisor circuits stored at the heart of the big machine. This last was mainly inquisitiveness: the computer was in some ways a mirror of his own powers, and he simply wanted to know it better; but there was also the practical point that the supervisor circuits allotted priorities to all computations demanded of the big machine from consoles all over the building. They did this partly on the basis of the work involved in each demand, but partly on the importance in the hierarchy of the man who made the demand. Humayan saw no harm in working himself a few rungs up that invisible ladder.

That evening there was a further note on his door: "Sir, I *must* clean your room. Herself has given the order." He was trying to think of a firm but placating choice of phrase, which would not involve his taking the argument to Mrs. Glister, when a door opened on the far side of the landing.

"I bet it wasn't like that," said Glenda. "I bet Moirag simply asked Mum if she was supposed to, and Mum said yes without thinking. I wonder what she's up to— I have to clean my room, because she persuaded Mum it was character-forming."

"I do not wish to trouble your mother."

"Tell Moirag to go and jump in the lake then."

"I cannot do that."

"Which was why I suggested it. What are you having for supper?"

"I have bought a tin of sardines and a tin of baked beans."

"Slurp, slurp. Is there enough for two? It's ages till our supper and school lunch was ugh."

"Come in," said Humayan uneasily. He unlocked his door and took the inadequate tins from his briefcase. He was hungry too.

"It's OK," said Glenda. "I'll nick some bread and bananas out of our kitchen. I'll cook and you can wash up."

Glenda was a noisy cook, a banger, scraper and rattler. It took Humayan some time to realise that the new sound in the room was not emerging from the kitchen. As soon as he concentrated on it it became a man's voice, harsh and steady. Nor was it a harangue from the gym-instructor; it came out of the cupboard. Kate had a man in her room, then, and he did not sound very pleased with her; it was impossible to imagine Doctor Glister addressing even the most errant daughter in those tones, minatory and implacable.

Glenda came out of the smoke-filled kitchen-box with a spatula in her hand and stood by the cupboard with her head cocked on one side. Carefully she eased the cupboard door open, and at once the voice became clear for whole phrases together: "... the logic of power ... I have received many letters ... clear evidence ... deliberate perversion of government statistics ... an alien presence ... Thames foaming with blood ..." Regardless of the apparent meaning of the words the voice continued its monotonous, crashing rhythm, a surf of oratory breaking on the shores of rocklike minds. Glenda shut the door.

"Stupid nit," she said. "Playing it that loud."

"What was it?"

"Where have you been—that's the Druid Enoc. You've heard of *him*."

"Enoc ap Hywel? The Welsh leader? But he is in prison, surely?"

"They got him out three months ago—where *have* you been?"

"In India."

"Yes, but ... anyway, he's in Ireland now, and that's an illegal record Dad smuggled home. You can get three months for just listening to it, and a couple of years for simply owning a copy."

"But your neighbours would surely not report you."

"No, of course not. But it isn't like that. We're all super liberals, OK? But we can only go on being super

38

liberals and having super easy consciences provided nobody *does* anything. When Kate plays old Enoc that loud Mr. Ede is bound to hear it, next door, and start wondering what he's going to say when the RRB Conciliators come and ask him whether he heard anything: he says No and he's in trouble with the RRB, and that's *trouble*; he says Yes and he finds himself a witness at Dad's trial. Very unpleasant. It's in the contract of lease, I expect, that you can do what you like in the Yard provided you don't cause any unpleasantness. Do you want curry powder in your baked beans?"

"I am not fussy."

"You'd better not be, with me cooking. I should have put it in first, I suppose. Well, here goes."

She had fried some bread, sliced the bananas and added them with the curry powder to the baked beans, poured that mess over the fried bread and draped the warmed sardines across the top. The blue haze of her frying swirled through the room, as it used to in the eating-place of the sprawling Bombay flat where Humayan's mother's sister spent all day at the stove to be able to feed her luscious mushes to twenty hungry cousins. The sharp and sweet and oily mixture on his plate now was much to his taste, but Glenda suddenly took the savour out of it by saying, "Just like home, I bet."

His nape prickled and he found it difficult to swallow his mouthful. She had taken her glasses off to eat, which she had not done on the night of his arrival. Now he could see how strong was the cast in her left eye—a sure sign of a witch.

"It is very good," he managed to say. "I believe your other neighbour is a journalist."

"Frank? He's not quite as bad as the others—at least not that way. He writes for our sort of super liberal sort of paper, but he's a real yellow to talk to."

"Yellow?"

"Half-way to being green. He's Kate's boy-friend. You wanted her for yourself, I expect?"

She stopped eating and looked at him, smiling. Her

39

right eye held his, and her left seemed fixed on his forehead.

"I? Good gracious me, no."

"You can't have her, I'm afraid. Everybody wants Kate —even Dad, in his heart—but nobody can have her because she's dead gone on Frank. She's supposed to be looking for a job, but she's not trying very hard because Frank doesn't work mornings, and she likes to be about then."

She slid a sardine into her mouth in a deliberately meaningful way. A rush of thoughts stampeded through his mind: wondering what sort of man Mr. Francis Leary was; a mild disappointment, a familiar state, for he had had many disappointments in love and lust; residual hope, for the existence of one lover might provide a path for another, and Indian tales are full of episodes where one man impersonates another under cover of darkness; the waning of even that hope, with the certainty that Mr. Leary's stature was likely to be detectably different from his, be the night never so dark; and returning doubt whether Glenda's sardine had been as meaningful as he had supposed. She was very young. Perhaps she was just inventing excitements.

"I'm sorry about Kate," she said. "And you can't have me either—I'm saving myself up for the great Minus One when he becomes plus."

"But you will be minus then, surely?"

"Hell! Anyway, I'm going to kick Helen out of my church—she's a heretic. She sang 'Love Divine' all through prayers this morning, and when I ticked her off she said it was because she liked the tune. So she sang it in tune—or tried to. That's heresy, isn't it?"

"If you say so."

"Great. Well I do say so. Look, I'll go and nick that Enoc record, just so you can see it. Then when some super liberal tells you you don't know anything about the set-up here, you'll be able to say you've seen and heard an Enoc disc. There's not a lot of them about. I can't think where Dad picked it up."

He sat trembling on the bed. He understood now how

she did it. When she took her glasses off her squint allowed her left eye to look straight through his skull into his own third eye, which everyone knows is the gate of the soul. He prided himself on not being a superstitious man, and so was glad to have arrived at a scientific explanation for the phenomenon, but he was still trembling when she returned with the record.

It was like any other, except that a circle of white paper had been pasted over the original label, which in any case seemed to have been almost blank. Humayan turned it over in shaking hands, thinking that if the police or the Conciliators walked in now he would be liable for three months in prison. For politeness' sake he peered closely at the white round in the centre, and at one angle could see that the original had held a line of careful script, too small to decipher, and three larger stamped letters which might be three Bs. He was glad to hand it back to Glenda, and gladder still when she left.

The RRB had a strangely ill-balanced reference library. Many of the books were on locked shelves, but the Laboratory Controller supplied him with a special ticket entitling him to ask for the keys. He had formed a vague hypothesis which was just, he thought, worth a preliminary test and he wanted to see whether any usable figures were available for the previous expansion of the Green population, in the mid-nineteenth century, enough at least for him to construct a crude model and attempt a run-back. The books he needed seemed seldom to have been used, and the figures turned out to be hopeless guesses. But since he was down there he asked for and found a small shelf of books on British folklore, including several on witch cults.

Every word he read confirmed his guesses; even apparently random frivolities, like the great Minus One, fitted in. He made notes, and comforted himself with the thought that the large sum of money his father had spent on his horoscope had been fully justified. While he was reading an oddity on the table caught his eye. He had left a sheet of paper lying across the title-page of one of the books, half-obscuring the mark of the RRB stamp

41

so that only the tops of the three letters were exposed. They read, like that, as three Bs. So had the obscured stamp on the Druid Enoc's record. The thought of that disc drew his mind to Kate's room, and the reasons for her apathy over finding a job. He wondered whether she really did have a lover—certainly that might account for her look of lively delight. Luscious imaginings began to fill his mind, but the only physical effect on him was that his right eye started to weep most disconcertingly.

He put the books away, and during the lunch hour went round to India House and persuaded an official there to send a cable in Hindi to his mother, asking her to dispatch him, instanter, a very powerful charm against witches. The official was perfectly understanding, both of the need and of Humayan's wish that such a message should not pass through the machinery of this alien culture.

III

---

*THE CHANCELLOR OF THE EXCHEQUER: I agree
of course with the Hon. Member that Britain currently
enjoys the highest standard of living in the Western
World, but I totally reject the imputations in the phrase
'cheap Celtic Labour'. The Celtic section of our society
itself enjoys a far higher standard of living than any
similarly situated people with whom comparisons can
fairly be made. In terms of real income, for instance, the
Indian tribes of the Brazilian forests are immeasurably
worse off than ...*

Humayan met Moirag for the first time on Saturday
morning. He had made up his laundry-bundle and tidied
away his sparse breakfast while the Hoover was mumbling
at other carpets, and by the time it had reached Kate's
bedroom he had spread an array of papers across the
little table and littered a few books round the floor.
So he was ready for her.

Even so he jumped at the sharp rapping on the door,
though he was conscious of his own rectitude: Mrs.
Glister paid this ignorant woman good wages, so it would
be immoral to collude in her wasting her time watching
Kate Glister and her lover through the spyhole. He was
a hard-working intellectual, and it was only just that the
lower orders of society should work equally hard at their
far simpler tasks. His eye was still rather sore, so he put

his sunglasses on before opening the door at the second rattle of knocking.

She was a large woman, though hardly two inches taller than himself. But her breadth was prodigious, her hair as orange as a carrot, her face a viridian slab. Even his sunglasses did not diminish the shock of colour.

"*Now* I'll be cleaning your room ... sir," she announced. Her voice was deep, resonant and triumphant.

"My room is clean, thank you," said Humayan. "And I am working."

He stood slightly aside to let her see the panorama of papers, but she took the movement for an invitation to enter and he had to prance back into the doorway. They stood thus, chest to chest, so close that he could smell the brandy on her breath. Her look was queenly.

"I must do my cleaning," she said. "I know what my duty is."

"I have cleaned the rooms myself, and I must not have my papers disturbed."

"Herself gives the orders."

"I will speak to Mrs. Glister."

"I have spoken to her ... sir. I have my orders."

She leaned forward slightly so that the enormous bulge of her bosom pressed against him. He knew at once he was fighting out of his weight.

"Can't you see I am working?" he said shrilly.

She sniffed derision.

"My work is important. It is for the Race Relations Board!"

The blankness of her face convulsed.

"You! Ye thowless wee blackamoor!"

"You are not to speak to me in such terms," he shouted. "I will not endure it! I will report ..."

Her jaw worked. A yellow gob of spittle exploded from her lips and landed on the gold carpet at his feet. As she turned away he found he was screaming at her vast back in Hindustani. He was only able to stop when Kate's gold head came floating into view as she ran lightly up the stairs.

"Is everything all right?" she said in a bewildered voice. Moirag almost barged her down the stairs, but

44

she clung to the banisters. Humayan pulled himself back into his present culture.

"It is nothing serious," he said stiffly. "We had a misunderstanding over the cleaning of my room."

"Oh, that's all right," said Kate vaguely. "I expect Moirag will do it in the end."

With a smile of relief she went into her own room, looking divinely pink and blissful. Humayan was intrigued to notice that she locked the door. He did the same, and put the key on his table before opening the window. He hoped that this might equalise the draught through the spyhole. The gym-instructor was roaring at a class to get their knees up, and that too was an advantage, as it might muffle any inadvertent noises Humayan happened to make in the cupboard—sighings, groanings, or the like.

He had a long wait, and the longer it lasted the more puzzled he became. His initial puzzle was how Moirag had managed to fit her bulk into this cramped cuboid, but on reflection he decided that it was possible. She evidently had a powerful will. His second puzzle was how she had expected to spin out her supposed cleaning of the room for so long; his wait stretched on and on. He looked at times through the spyhole, for the draught was distinctly less now; Kate was restless, but not in a fashion that suggested that her lover was late. She lay for some time on her stomach on the bed, reading a magazine, so that he could admire the swelling of her neatly trousered buttocks. Out of his line of vision her wireless gibbered pop; at last, when a voice was singing croakily that its heart was in the highlands, dad, the man came. He knew this because the sound was switched off while she still lay on the bed, though she had turned and was smiling towards the window. She got off her bed, and in that instant the man must have shut the window, for the draught became agonising. She walked out of his line of vision.

"Bend!" roared the gym-instructor. "Further! Further! Hold it!"

He dared not retreat and shut his own window (a) for fear of making a noise, (b) because it might suddenly

45

muffle the sound of the gym-instructor's bellowings, (c) because the man might have seen it open as he came along the ledge. They were a long time out of sight. Humayan was beginning to wonder what he was missing when the man suddenly strolled into the arc commanded by the spyhole; he stood and lit a cigarette, then turned back towards the window so that Humayan could study his profile. He was wearing yellow pyjamas. He was tall, with a longish red face ending in an untidy brown beard; premature baldness heightened his brow; he was certainly not handsome, but in its coarse, big-featured fashion his look was one of energy and drive. While he stood there Kate, still (Humayan was glad to see) fully dressed, came and nestled against him, sliding her hands to and fro over his back. Knowing her height, Humayan was able to gauge his. He was a big man, indeed. He patted her haunches with his free hand and gazed out over her head at the window, though there was nothing to see there but the yellow brick wall from beyond which the gym-instructor bellowed his monotonous numbers. The draught through the spyhole became so painful that Humayan had to close his eye and withdraw it. He willed himself not to look again until he had counted sixty.

Kate was lying on the bed now, unbuttoning her blouse with slow care. The man, still smoking, sat on the bed beside her with his back to the spyhole. He did not seem very interested in Kate, fondling her thigh without much attention, much as Mrs. Glister had fondled the ears of one of her dogs while she had told Humayan how badly the young behaved these days. His large red hand ran in slow arcs across the rounded limb. There was something wrong with the fingers, but through the mists of the martyring draught Humayan couldn't see quite what. The man stubbed his cigarette out and as if that had been a signal Kate cast herself upwards with a sudden convulsion, like a fish leaping from the water, and pulled him down. Humayan could hear his laugh as he came. Then the eye demanded another thirty seconds of relief.

"Ready now?" bellowed the gym-instructor. Humayan sprang back to attention at the spyhole.

46

It was perfectly maddening. The man was not ready. Really he had the most enviable self-restraint. Kate had let him go and had sat up to slip out of her trousers, but the man's bulk still screened her as he yawningly removed his yellow pyjamas. The steady welling of tears made the scene slip in and out of focus as the drops concentrated and dispersed. The man's back was white but muscular, and heavily scarred in two places. Down by the waistline was a single silvery slash, and up on the left shoulder-blade a curious, puckered, branching knot of spoilt tissue. Again Kate tried to pull him down, but this time, effortlessly, he lifted her to him and held her close. For a moment Humayan thought that they intended to perform the act in a sitting position—he had not read that the English were as imaginative as that— but no, it was just more fondlings. Humayan began to be aware that soon he himself would no longer be able to maintain the objective detachment which is the hall-mark of the scientific observer. Ah, when would they begin? He closed his agonising eye.

At that moment chill fingers gripped his wrist. He shrivelled, then slowly turned his head.

Glenda, grinning, was beckoning him into his room. He summoned a little dignity and obeyed. Silent as a tree-snake she took his place, but only stayed a few seconds before emerging, still grinning, but like a death's-head now. She closed the door with care.

"I want to talk to you," she whispered.

"I have work to do."

"And laundry. We can talk at the launderette."

The gym-instructor began to bellow the steady rhythm of his numbers. "One-ah! Two-ah! Three-ah! Fooouuurrr! One-ah! ..."

Humayan picked his bundle of laundry off the bed, telling himself that he had intended to take it up the road before long, and so was in no way diminishing his own freedom of action by acceding to Glenda's request. They let themselves out of his room like thieves. As he locked the door he saw Glenda putting the spare key of his room away in her purse-belt. She was not in school uniform today, but wearing a black-and-red-striped rugby

47

zephyr and red bell-bottomed trousers. Her feet were bare.

The green attendants stayed in the furthest corner of the launderette, a sluttish, chain-smoking trio. One pale student, reading a biography of Cromwell, sat waiting for his wash; several other machines churned for absentee launderers. Glenda said nothing till his own shirts and under-clothes were revolving steadily and the white tide of suds had risen to its proper level.

"Now you can tell me your real name," she said.

"Certainly not. There is no reason why I should."

"Well, I could tell Kate you'd made a peephole into her room. She'd tell Frank, because she tells him everything. Frank likes hurting people. He really does."

Humayan remembered the tough, scarred back, the half-brutal boredom of the man's love-making.

"This is ridiculous," he said.

"All right. I expect I'll see you."

She rose, smiling.

"My name is Pravandragasharatipili Humayan," he whispered.

"You'll have to write it down. I'll borrow a biro from one of those Greens."

As she bossed the trio of attendants into putting themselves out for her he considered the advantages of spelling his name wrong. No. She would find out. She would know. She knew everything. When she came back he wrote it down for her in careful capitals and coached her in the proper pronunciation.

"Great," she said. "Pravandragasharatipili. But I'll still call you Pete, except ... Look, I've got a present for you. I want you to wear this."

She fidgeted under the sleeve of her zephyr and slid a bracelet down over her wrist. No, not a bracelet, he had seen exactly that strap of studded red leather before, round the necks of Want and Ought.

"I am not your dog!" he said angrily.

"Frank," she said, smiling and patting the purse-belt where the folded paper with his name lay hidden. "You can wear it under your sleeve and no one will know. It's a spare—Mum bought a puppy last year from Cousin Ranulph, but the other two ate it."

He turned the collar over in his hands. There was a little brass nameplate next to the buckle. It said 'Must'.

"This is all very childish," he muttered.

"In that case why are you making such a fuss about it?"

At its widest hole the collar fitted comfortably round his left forearm, where it was hidden by his shirtcuff. It felt at once as though he had always worn it.

"I suppose you'll have to take it off in the bath," said Glenda. "Do you think he really loves her?"

"How can I tell?"

"You're a man. But I suppose ... She loves *him*. She likes what he does to her. *I* couldn't ... anyway, I don't think he loves her. She's just a nice handy screw, who he doesn't even have to dress up for."

"The nature of men..." began Humayan.

"He doesn't love her. That's settled. Now, what do you make of this?"

She took the biro from him and on another scrap of paper drew a vertical line with a number of smaller lines crossing it at different angles. He studied it and shrugged.

"I may have got it wrong," she said. "It's the mark on Frank's shoulder. I think it's a brand, like cowboys do on cattle."

His eye began to weep again at the memory, but he made the necessary effort of recall and drew the scar as he thought he had seen it.

"My visual memory is not like my memory for numbers," he said apologetically; at once he was cross with himself for falling so quickly into the mistress-servant relationship she demanded.

"Yes, that's more like it," said Glenda. "I've seen that sort of mark..."

"Were you finished with me pen, then?" said a sharp voice.

"Thank you," said Glenda, holding up the biro without looking up. A green fist snatched the paper from her other hand.

49

"Boyo!" said the woman. "Not in here you don't! Out!"

"Do you know what it means?" said Glenda placidly. "It's quite like those sort of marks you see..."

The woman interrupted her, without saying anything more, simply by a movement. She slammed the scrap of paper down on the nearest washing machine and ground the stub of her cigarette into it. The acrid prickle of scorched paper pierced the fluffy detergent odours of the place. Her look was of sharp contempt, mixed with the older hatred of one race for its enemy race.

"The brown boyo can git, now," she said. "Or I'll call the boss and he'll call the cops. You can stay for the washing, lady—and then not be coming back."

"OK," said Glenda. "Sorry about that, Pete. Wait for me outside."

This was the broad, sloping avenue down which he had lugged his suitcase on Tuesday. Though it was now Saturday, the weekend, when even the most menial white was presumably slouched at home in front of the telly with the day's first beer-cans, the same street-sweeper was still on duty, shuffling up the gutter pushing the same pile of litter. Humayan saw now how tall he was, and young, and intellectual-looking, though all three factors were disguised by his melancholy stoop over his brush, or over his cart when he slouched back down the pavement to fetch it. Humayan's few direct dealings with Greens—Moirag, and now this angry woman in the launderette—had shown him that for a race of servants their manner was far from servile. He felt that he was destined to go back to India having learnt very little about them—little from his statistical research at the RRB, still less from the community in Horseman's Yard. His knowledge of the racially mixed society of Bombay University had shown him that there are no Europeans so ignorant of India as those who believe that they know it through their servants.

He was still staring at the man when Glenda joined him. They both started to speak together, he in vague terms about the unknowability of Greens, she about

50

something else. They paused for each other, and in that pause they felt and heard the judder of air that came from a distant explosion. Faces all down the pavement gazed east-south-east. Only the green sweeper seemed not to have noticed the disturbance.

"If that's Harrods again," said Glenda, "Mum will blow her top."

Humayan shrugged. It was no business of his.

"They're getting nearer," she said. "First it was Scotland and Wales, and then places like Liverpool. Now it's London. I wonder how long it'll be before they reach Horseman's Yard."

He took the paper bag from her and fussed through his clean linen.

"Is it all there?" he said. "How can you be sure?"

She laughed, and forgot about bombs.

"Of course it is," she said. "I'm going to look after you now. That's part of the deal. For instance I'll see Dad asks you to tomorrow's Committee ... oh, you'll enjoy it ... Sundays, provided it's fine, all the Yard gets together and has drinks before lunch. The idea is they can settle any problems that have come up, but really it's an excuse for a booze-up. You'd like to meet Frank with his clothes on, wouldn't you. I wonder what the hell she made such a fuss about in there over his scar—you used to see that sort of mark chalked up in all sorts of places. Not so much now, though."

Humayan shrugged and walked with her down the avenue. It was another of those problems which was his only in so far as it was hers.

He lunched alone in his room, then worked. At first the intricate abstractions of mathematical thought were merely a refuge from this savage culture where bombs exploded in the distance and servants spat at his feet and a young witch rode his shoulders; but after two hours, when he eased his buttocks, rubbery with stillness, to a new position, he found that the fingers of his right hand had for who knows how long past been steadily numbering off the nine brass studs on the collar round his left wrist, as a priest numbers the rotations of his prayer-

51

wheel. The process seemed to help his thought, and now he pursued it consciously. In the next two hours he untangled one statistical knot that had been puzzling him for weeks, and was able to pull that little thread of reasoning out clear. It was not an important thread, but he could not have proceeded far with the knot still there. Perhaps, he thought, Glenda was not a *bad* witch; she had meant it when she said she would look after him.

At length the blank stupor that follows such work overcame him. At home he would either have visited a brothel or taken his mother to the cinema, but the morning's drama had for the moment taken all relish out of either activity, so he decided to clean his room. He had bought dusters and a cheap brush and pan, and Moirag had left him a legacy of dirt that made its removal a satisfying achievement. He shifted the meagre furniture about to get at areas which had been unswept for years; the disturbed dust hung in the air like smoke. When he was in the furthest corner of the room, which was normally covered by the bed, his brushing was impeded by a slight rectangular rise in the carpet. The tacks had been removed, too, and never hammered back, so he was able to turn the flap of carpet over and find a yellow Kodak envelope with a dozen photographic prints in it. He sat on the bed to look at them.

The first two were indecipherable misty greys; the third showed a shape he recognised, partly because the blurring was much the same as the blurring in his vision when he had peered through the spyhole—it was part of Kate's bed and her bedside table. The fourth, now he knew what to look for, was two naked bodies on the bed; the fifth Mr. Leary's profile; the sixth his back, with the brand or scar on it quite plain; the rest were all pictures of Kate and her lover, snapped through the spyhole, neither erotic nor informative. Because Glenda was interested Humayan made a careful sketch of the brand, then put the prints back in their envelope and that into a larger one on which he wrote the one word 'Moirag'. He left this in the kitchen when he went out for his evening stroll.

This time he walked south, through a well-appointed district, tall houses on either side of broad streets, their white paint shining in the slant sunlight; the parked cars were large and new; well-dressed children were being shepherded home from some playground by spruce nannies whose nunnish uniforms set off their young figures and gave a prim but kindly look to the withdrawn green faces. Most of these children were European, but some were yellow and brown—scions, presumably, of the diplomatic bag. Behind certain of the nannies strolled pairs of men, sober-suited, square-shouldered and alert, usually with one hand in a jacket pocket.

London smelt of summer dust and money, but hardly at all of people and their dirt. It was not like any city Humayan had ever known. He wandered at random until his way was blocked by a six-lane highway with a barrier-rail running all its length, but not far to his right he saw what seemed to be a pedestrian subway, so he set off towards it. As he reached the top of the ramp he heard a shout of alarm from below; feet scampered and two green youths, thirteen-year-olds, came racing up towards him. Their ragged plimsolls flapped on the ramp as they raced past him without a glance; he watched them scramble over the barrier and jink through the hurtling traffic; from the far carriageways came the squeal of braked tyres and the wincing clash of metal and glass. Humayan walked hurriedly down the ramp, having no desire to waste his time by appearing as a witness in a traffic accident.

The subway was well-lit, but not clean, and pervaded by the smell of urine. Half-way along a couple of white policemen, armed, were studying the wall. There was a pot of paint by their feet. They looked up at the sound of Humayan's steps and waited for him to approach. He swallowed as he came.

"Card," said one of them gruffly.

Humayan opened his wallet and drew out his National Health Card. While the first policeman studied it the second said, "What do you know about this, then?"

His gesture indicated a horizontal black line on the wall, and the short lines, vertical and slanting, which crossed it in an irregular pattern for half its length. The paint was wet.

"Those marks?" said Humayan a little shrilly. "They have nothing to do with me! Two youths ran out shouting as I came into the tunnel."

"Two youths," said the second policeman tonelessly. He shifted his stance an inch, poised for a blow, but the first policeman shoved the card under his nose and flipped the top right-hand corner with a finger. The second policeman's brows rose.

"That's all right, sir," said the first policeman, handing the card back. "I see you have not been long in our country then?"

"Just a week."

"I see, sir. Well, the road here is a Zone border. I'm afraid I must ask you to go back the way you came, sir."

"Of course, of course," said Humayan, determined to show himself a good Saxon citizen. "Can you please tell me what the marks mean?"

"*I* can't read the stuff," growled the second policeman, as though he were a circus animal suddenly asked to perform an impossible trick. "But whatever it means it's IRH."

"Incitement to Racial Hatred, sir," translated the first policeman. "Good day, sir."

Humayan walked up the ramp, puzzling why someone had chosen to brand a white journalist's shoulder-blade with an incitement to racial hatred. The traffic in the further lanes was now at a standstill, with police bikes threading their way through towards the obstructing clot. White men stood round their cars, pointing and arguing. Four or five cars had achieved union in metal. A breakdown van, orange light flashing, came surging up from the other direction and a policeman halted the traffic in the near lanes to allow it through an opening in the central barrier. Now that all the cars were still Humayan could see the scene of the crash more clearly; close to the foremost of the shunted cars lay a dark, sack-like object from which one green arm projected at an impossible angle. One of the arguing drivers gestured to-

54

wards it, as if to prove a point, but no one else paid any attention to the dead boy.

Humayan found Doctor Glister in the hall, wreathed in smoke but bright-eyed.

"Ah, Pete," he said between sucks. "I was hoping to see you. The good folk who live in the Yard have a get-together on Sunday mornings, before lunch, and I thought you might care to come and have a look at them."

"And allow them to have a look at me?" The encounter with the policemen, and to a lesser extent the death of the young slogan-writer, had made Humayan suddenly a little prickly about his place in this Western culture, whatever his card proclaimed him to be.

"Yes, yes," said Doctor Glister, blinking. "They are all ... well ... pretty *intelligent* people, I'm glad to say."

Humayan made the obvious translation to 'broad-minded'.

"I will be delighted to attend," he said.

"Good, good," said Doctor Glister and then just stood there, wheezing at his pipe like some machine which is not being used for its real function but whose engine is allowed to idle on.

"I have been puzzled by some marks I have seen on walls," said Humayan.

"Uh-huh?"

"May I draw the sort of thing?"

On the tiny table in the hall lay a memo pad and a silver pencil. Most of the space on the pad was taken up by the words 'Try to Remember' and a cartoon of a smug woman in furs leading a dachshund with a knot tied in its middle, but there was room for a rough representation of the marks in the subway. Doctor Glister frowned at the paper and sucked his pipe so hard that it emitted a musical note; then he rolled the paper into a spill, lit it with a match and went through a charade of using the spill to re-light his already fuming pipe.

"Saves matches," he said, moving back a couple of paces so that he could glance into the kitchen. "Ogham, an ancient Irish script which our idiot government has

55

made it illegal to use, teach or refer to. It's not bad for slogans, but too clumsy for anything else. I understand that it developed from a secret sign-language of the druids, based on the Greek alphabet, with one to five fingers held in various positions to indicate twenty letters. The script is just a rough representation of those finger positions. Where did you see this?"

The final question, after the hypnotically mumbled explanation, was almost inaudible but the glance was very sharp. Humayan told his story, omitting the accident in case Doctor Glister was sufficiently public-spirited —at least vicariously—to feel that he should have offered himself as a witness after all.

"Yes, yes," said Doctor Glister, losing interest. "But they wouldn't have turned you back if you'd shown them your RRB pass."

"I do not have one."

"Oh, but you ought to!"

Doctor Glister took his pipe out of his mouth to say this, and said it with a sudden shocked concern, as though Humayan were on the verge of committing some ugly social solecism. Then he put his pipe back and reverted to mumbles.

"What I mean is, however detestable our regime, it is foolish not to arm oneself with the weapons it actually provides. Don't you agree?"

His look was still very sharp, as though he were searching for some sign that Humayan had seen through his bufferish mask. Or perhaps the look itself was just another mannerism, like the blinks and the pipe-sucking. Humayan thanked him and went upstairs.

He did not feel like cooking his own evening meal, and he felt lonely and alien, so he decided to go and investigate an Indian restaurant, Saxons only, which he had seen in the course of his walk. Witch or no witch, the planets were still smiling on him, for the proprietor, Mr. Palati, came from Bombay, was of Humayan's own caste, and took his trade seriously. He neglected his other customers to gossip with Humayan, and before the evening was out gave him the address of a club for Indians in London, and also of two reliable brothels.

56

"And of course, my dear fellow," he added, "you will not go chasing the green ladies. Oh no. The English are very superstitious about such things, I tell you often I have laughed at their ignorances, and they believe the green ladies have special talents, you know? But I can promise you from my own experience it is not so, all lies and fantasies, and now the law has made the punishments very severe, very horrible. Only the English would be fools enough to take such risks. But there is a fat white girl at the Daffodil who can..."

Mr. Palati made her sound very exotic, but Humayan, to his alarm, felt no stirrings.

And even next morning, Sunday, when the gym was quiet and the far traffic stilled and he could detect certain faint movements beyond the cupboard, he felt no particular urge to inspect. This alarmed him still more. He turned his book over, closed his eyes and whispered those verses of the *Kama Sutra* that had never before failed to bring him to bursting manhood, if he chose. The charm had no effect.

This was Glenda's doing. He remembered her look as she had come from the cupboard and a broken phrase in the launderette. Yes, she hated the sex act, so she had bound her new servant...

Scrabbling with terror he began to unbuckle the collar from his wrist, and then an opposite and equal terror stopped him. What kind of curse might an English witch have put on such a token? Wait! She had said he could take it off in the bath!

In the tiny shower-space, with the warm water slashing its whips against his shoulders, the *Kama Sutra* worked its boyhood magic. He sang a little as he dried. The thought had struck him that Mr. Palati might know of a house where the girls were prepared to offer their services in a showerbath. London, after all, is a mighty city, catering for many needs. And thanks to the majestic salary that the RRB was paying him he could afford such amenities.

He chose seven minutes past twelve as the precise

moment to make his appearance in the courtyard. Little groups of pale people stood about among the vivid flower-pots; he felt the flicker of all their eyes as he stole forth, and heard a judder in the conversation like a bad cut in a taped radio conversation; then the eyes switched back and the fluting tones of Kensington rippled on. Moirag and another green maid were handing round drinks; three middle-aged men in expensive casuals were talking to Kate, almost nudging each other for her attention; she was laughing, but not at anything any of them had said. Humayan thought it lovely to see her standing there in the noon sunshine, flowering with happiness, however base a dung had fed the flower. He considered this a very poetical image, and that it was particularly generous of him to think of it, considering all the circumstances. Glenda was talking to Kate's lover, who wore a rather old brown shirt and brown trousers; she waved and beckoned him over, but Doctor Glister intercepted him.

"Hello there," he said. "What'll you drink, Pete? Just orange? Sure? No, no, that's no trouble ... Moirag, will you be squeezing an orange for Mr. Humayan, darlint?"

Moirag scowled assent.

"Fine, fine," said Doctor Glister. "Now, Pete, let's find you someone who isn't talking about bombs and kid-nappings. Who would you like to meet? And—don't say it—who would like to meet you? What about these three lovely ladies?"

Two of the lovely ladies, Mrs. French and Mrs. Smith-Higgins, were of roughly the same age as Mrs. Glister but less handsome, the former being short and red-faced and the latter a pale, harsh creature with grey and wispy hair. The third, Mrs. Turnbull, was young and brisk and buxom, with hair drawn hard back in a bun. From time to time a small boy rushed through the crowd of drinkers and swung on her skirt as though he were try-ing to pull it down, but it had been engineered to with-stand such stresses.

"But don't you *think*," she was saying with a braying note on the emphasised words, "it was a very wicked feature to attempt *at all*? I mean, we're all glad to *know*, but ..."

"What are you talking about, Polly darling?" said Doctor Glister.

"The witch report," snapped Mrs. Turnbull. Humayan jumped and shrank at the same moment. Now that Glenda had tamed him, was the whole coven about to reveal itself?

"Oh, I don't know," twittered Mrs. French. "Personally I thought it was all jolly interesting and . . ."

"One moment, Mary," said Mrs. Smith-Higgins. "Mr. Humayan hasn't the faintest notion what we're talking about, and how could he?"

Her attempt to pronounce his name in a thoroughly foreign fashion was gallant but misconceived. Mrs. Turnbull sighed with impatience to return to her tirade, but Doctor Glister, however soft his intonation, was a more experienced conversation-snatcher.

"Yes, Pete," he said. "We have here a magazine called *Which?* whose life's work is to protect the interest of the consumer, and to measure the different excellencies and failings—mostly failings—of goods and services. One month it will tell you that so-and-so's children's bikes fall to bits on their first outing, and the next that the cheapest soap contains exactly the same ingredients as the most expensive. Never shall I forget the rejoicing among the bourgeoisie when *Which?* pronounced what they all already knew, that Sainsbury's was the best chain foodstore. It was as though Christ had appeared to the apostles and told them that two and two make four. So what have they done this month, Polly? I had thought you were their staunchest defender."

"Usually, yes," snapped Mrs. Turnbull. "But this month they've done *servants*. They've got about a thousand stupid bitches up and down the country to fill in forms about their servants, and tabulated the results, as if they were electric *kettles*! I *ask* you!"

"And the Welsh came out on top, easily, of course," said Mrs. French. "Gwynnedd was frightfully pleased when I told her."

"Pleased enough to be drunk all evening," said Mrs. Turnbull. "We could hear her singing all through *Hedda Gabler*."

"But she's got a beautiful voice," protested Mrs. French. "That's another advantage, only there wasn't anywhere for it on the form."

"As a matter of fact," said Mrs. Smith-Higgins with fastidious clarity, "I don't agree with either of you. I can see no harm in doing the survey, provided it's properly done. But this was ridiculous—not just the silly cartoons they printed with it, but such a small sample, and the control group of European *au pairs* even smaller, and so many loaded questions. For instance that one about illegitimate babies, where the Greens came out with a far higher ratio than the *au pairs*..."

"Well, we all knew *that*," said Mrs. French.

"...but they didn't make any allowance for the difficulty of Greens getting free contraception, especially in white Zones, and they didn't..."

"Sue!" said Mrs. Turnbull with a different sharpness in her voice. Humayan felt the lovely ladies' eyes flick over him. He smiled a meek apology for his untrustworthiness.

"Oh, Pete's all right," said Doctor Glister. "In fact this is just his cup of tea. He's a professional statistician."

Having injected this numbing dart into the conversation he turned away. Moirag came stumping across the yard with a tumbler of orange juice which she thrust gruffly at Humayan, but Mrs. Turnbull stopped him from taking it.

"Moirag!" she said briskly. "That glass is perfectly filthy. Get him a clean one."

The criticism was justified. Mauve lipstick smeared one rim of the glass and lip-shaped crescents of milk the other. Moirag grunted and wheeled away.

"I'm sorry," said Mrs. Smith-Higgins. "It's just one of those things."

"One is very much on their side, of course," agreed Mrs. Turnbull, "but it's stupid to pretend they aren't often quite impossible."

"That's what I was saying," said Mrs. Smith-Higgins. "People keep telling us we live in an age of communications, but they always leave out that communications only work if they're true. The whole truth. Things like this *Which?* report—if you leave out the marriage and residence regulations because of the RRB, then you..."

Humayan had been vaguely aware that a man had drifted into their group. Now the newcomer spoke.

"Sue darling, come and talk to Denny and Toby about finances for the nativity play."

The newcomer was bronzed but flabby. He laid a ringed hand on Mrs. Smith-Higgins's arm and she stopped with her mouth open.

"Hell, we've only just finished the accounts for the last one," she said.

He smiled and explained, not to his wife but the other three.

"They're off to Malaga next week, and when they come back it will be almost summer hols."

His hand now gripped her skinny arm. Humayan saw a definite tug, and a moment of resistance, before he led her away.

"*Not* a very good excuse," said Mrs. Turnbull.

"But just in time," twittered Mrs. French. "Poor darling Sue, it's such hell for her sticking our company for an hour that she has two or three quick ones before she comes out."

"It must be hell, being no good at people, like that," said Mrs. Turnbull.

"There you are," said Mrs. French, "that's a nice clean glass, Mr. Humayan."

And it was. But Moirag had stirred at least a dessert-spoonful of salt into the orange. He was shocked to discover that the idiot feud still continued, but he sipped the appalling mixture and wondered what he could do to end it while he half-listened to Mrs. Turnbull and Mrs. French analysing the importance of being good at people, their arguments all based on their own virtues and tacit reservations about each other's. Then Kate slipped in beside him.

"Hi, Polly," she said. "Hello, Mrs. F. Do you mind if I take Pete away? Francis wants to talk to him."

Any demur they made was invisible. Humayan bowed to them, and as he was doing so was nearly flung to the floor by a buffet from behind. He recovered and looked

61

round to see Moirag surging away, taking no more notice of the collision than an oil-tanker might which ran down a row-boat. Kate too was unconcerned, and led him across the courtyard, smiling off several male attempts to suck her into conversations. Humayan could almost feel the prickle of inner gaiety like static electricity around her. When she introduced her lover she lingered over the syllables of his name, in an attempt to suggest mysterious Erse diphthongs.

"And Pete's is even worse," she said. "It's got eighteen syllables so he lets us call him Pete."

"Very decent of him," said Mr. Leary. His face was broader than that glance at his profile had suggested, and its redness was not the flush of health or high blood-pressure, but a curious weathering of the skin as though it had been scrubbed a few days earlier for too long a time with too harsh a brush. His nose had a drooping, smashed-in-childhood shape, so his whole countenance seemed coarse and battered and debauched, except that his blue eyes were not at all bloodshot. He spoke with an educated accent, occasionally softening a vowel so that 'decent' was half-way to 'dacint'.

"Katie says you're working in my field," he said.

"I am not sure what your field comprises," said Humayan, who was beginning to wish that he had been less free with his vauntings about his discoveries and prowess.

"The whole green world is my pasture," said Mr. Leary. " 'Green' with a capital 'g' of course. I am paid to be tender with the susceptibilities of minority groups. Hi, kid sister."

Glenda thrust between them a plate of little biscuits soggy with paté.

"Now listen," she said. "You treat Pete right or I'll do you."

She slid away, a knack of movement she had inherited from her father.

"She scares me," said Mr. Leary with a laugh. "She has a will of iron and she knows too much. Mind if I call you Pete too? Fine. Now the point is I work for *The* ... hell, anyway, you probably won't know it, but it's a newspaper. I'm their Celtic Affairs Correspondent. Anything green is my meat. I write under the name of Frank Lear to preserve our reputation for impartiality. That's the sort of paper we are—editorial staff soft liberal, shareholders hard fascist. We compromise..."

"Ah, the British genius," said Humayan.

"The English genius. We devote a lot of shocked space to Celtic affairs, and keep the shareholders—*and* the censors—happy by never breathing one hint that anything whatever could be done to improve things, except for the worse. So you'll be a bit of a change, if Katie's got it right. You've made a breakthrough about the green gene, and that landed you a job with the RRB. Right?"

"In very general terms, but ... oh, it is difficult for a foreigner like me. I am beginning to think that when I first landed in your country I spoke too freely about my work. I do not know..."

"Sure, sure. You'd have to get an OK from R14—that's Dick Mann's outfit—before you gave me an interview, and Dick'd want to vet my story afterwards. The RRB is very hot on that sort of thing. But it'd be a spot of publicity for you. That never did any harm to a young scientist with his toes on the first rungs of the ladder, huh?"

This was a very true observation. To be a household word, to have a sheaf of press-cuttings to show—oh not to the scientists on the selection committees, but perhaps to lay vice-chancellors and local businessmen who hold the purse-strings ... But Humayan was still uneasy.

"You'll be going to the office tomorrow?" said Mr. Leary.

"Yes, naturally."

"OK, you go along to R14 and see what they think. I'll give them a ring first thing, so they'll know what you're talking about. My bet is they'll jump at it—here they are, beavering away at the great Celtic Problem, bringing foreign geniuses half the way round the world to help; why shouldn't people hear about it? Then if it's clear with them you can nip round to my place when you come home—six too early?—and we'll do a proper interview in peace and quiet, with no mikes in the flower-

63

pots. Save me going to *my* office, unless some hothead blows up Buck House or kidnaps the French Embassy chef. See you then, then."

He nodded and lounged off. Before Humayan could attach himself to another group for their inspection Glenda stole up beside him. Her plate of horrible little eatables was almost empty.

"You have done good trade," he said.

"Buggers have their uses. Look."

She flicked one of the biscuits sideways off the plate. There was a scurry of tiny limbs among the drinkers' ankles and Want, or it might be Ought, gulped the morsel down.

"What did he want?" she whispered. "What did he want?"

Humayan glanced up at the basket of lobelias that dangled above his head. Was it conceivable that an RRB microphone nestled in the sopping peat?

"He wishes to interview me," he murmured. "But I do not..."

"No! You've got to do it!"

"Oh, why?"

"Find out more about him. When we've really got him taped we'll do him!"

"Oh?"

"Sneaking into our house, treating us like a brothel —and he doesn't even love her!"

Her hissing whisper was barely audible through the rattle of chatter. With a gesture of repulsion she tossed another biscuit down, and again the depraved little dogs pounced; but in mid-gulp the one who had snatched the morsel was retchingly sick, smothering a whole flagstone with bile-mingled crumbs and paté.

The drinkers on the further side of this embarrassment took a second or two to notice what had happened, because they were busy with speculation about the fate of some hostage, but then a stooping young giant called an order, the group shuffled a few feet away, and a green maid emerged with a bucket and cloth and knelt to gather up the vomit.

"Come and meet Denny and Toby," said Glenda.

"They're our two Christian queers. They might try to nobble you to play Balthazar in their nativity play, if you're still here at Christmas. It's a zoned church now, so Dad has to green up to play McCaspar."

IV

---

*THE MINISTER FOR ARTS (Lord Ealing): I welcome
the Noble Lord's enquiry as it gives me the opportunity
to clarify a point over which our country's reputation
for even-handed justice has been seriously and unfairly
impugned. I cannot assert too strongly that the Arts
Council Grants are distributed with absolute impartiality between the Celtic and Saxon sections of our community, bearing in mind the differing financial demands
of different arts. That last clause is the vital one. It so
happens that the Saxon culture covers a wider range of
artistic endeavour than the Celtic culture. Painting,
sculpture and all the visual arts have become increasingly
expensive in our day, while the verbal and musical arts
in which the Celts traditionally excel have remained
comparatively cheap.*
LORD LLANFECHAN: What about opera, bach?
*LORD EALING: I was not aware that Bach wrote
opera.* (Laughter.)

R14 was like any other official department, almost. The
reek of bureaucracy, so familiar to Indian nostrils, hung
there strong. Only the grey-haired women who occupied
the enquiry office were more smiling and polite than
usual—the one who dealt with his two requests apologised
gracefully when she showed him into a little side-cubicle
and told him there would be a short wait. And the chairs
in the cubicle were comfortable and the magazines up to
date.

And the wait was preternaturally short. Humayan had hardly opened next month's *Prism* when the woman came back and led him through several large offices where clerks toiled at the endless harvest of documents and into a plush vestibule where a younger woman rose smiling from behind a small telephone switchboard.

"This is Mr. P. Humayan," said the first woman, pronouncing it right. "I sent an H$_{12}$ through just now."

"That's right," said the second woman, smiling the same bland smile. "Please come this way, Mr. Humayan."

He thanked his old guide and followed the new one. In the next office a handsome young man was reading from a computer print-out into his telephone; the message appeared to concern a complex accumulator on that afternoon's racing at Newcastle. He kissed his hand to the woman but appeared not to notice Humayan any more than if he had been her shadow. She opened another door and paused just inside; a male voice answered her query; she ushered Humayan in and left at once.

The office was in all ways nondescript, neither large nor small, neither rich nor spare. Only the view from the window was unexpectedly bleak, a wall as featureless as the one Humayan saw from his own room in Horseman's Yard. The man too looked nondescript, but being a man was not to be judged by the same instantaneous criteria one uses on rooms and views. He wore shirtsleeves; his tie was decorated with crossed cricket-bats and held in place by a cheap clip; he was pale and puffy, but somehow not unhealthily so; his hair had receded a little but was cut rather shorter than that of most Englishmen Humayan had met; he looked about forty-five.

"Come in, Mr. Humayan," he said. "I'm glad to meet you. I've heard a lot about you. Take a seat and tell me your problems. My name is Mann, Dick Mann, and I'm supposed to be in charge of personnel in this racket. I'm not the boss—you've met the Old Man, I think—but it's my job to see he isn't bothered with little problems. I'm a kind of trouble-shooter—if you're trouble, I shoot you, pow!"

His tone was jokey but his eyes were heavy with long thought and endless decisions.

"I hope I am not trouble," said Humayan. "I did not expect to have to bother a senior official."

"That's the spirit. And you needn't have, but I'd heard a lot about you and I wanted to meet you. Doc. Glister treating you OK, I hope."

"Indeed yes. He is a most considerate landlord. It was he who suggested I should apply for an RRB pass."

"Sod him. Anything to cause us trouble. Tarquin, is that pass for Mr. Humayan ready yet?"

The last words were spoken into thin air. Out of thin air a voice replied, "Coming up." A grey gadget that stood by Mr. Mann's elbow blinked a couple of lights, fizzed and coughed. Its sputum was a rectangle of plastic that shot across Mr. Mann's desk and stopped against a projecting slat of wood. Mr. Mann picked it up, looked at it casually and passed it across to Humayan.

He was delighted with the photograph, which made him look both less depraved and less innocent than others he had had taken. The pass carried a long number in computer figures, and then his own name: Pravandragasharatipili ('Peter') Humayan. Finally a certification of his status as an employee of the Race Relations Board. He hesitated between asking for a copy of the photograph to send to his mother, and asking how they had known about 'Peter', for he was still on formal terms with his colleagues in the Laboratory. Mr. Mann misunderstood the hesitation.

"Just the same as mine," he said, fishing a similar rectangle from the jacket that hung on the back of his chair. "Won't get you out of real trouble, but it'll make the ordinary cops think twice."

He tossed his own pass across. Humayan studied it politely; the code number began with a different set of digits, and the photograph was a few years old, taken at a time when Mr. Mann had possessed harder lines in his features and perhaps softer in his soul.

"Oh, I am quite satisfied," said Humayan, passing it back. "Thank you very much. You were extremely quick."

"Oh don't thank me—thank the big machine. My mate

68

down in the basement, you know. Does all my thinking for me."

"Yes," said Humayan, "that is a very impressive computer. The best I have ever worked with."

"Bloody well ought to be," said Mr. Mann. "What it cost us in dollars! There's only one like it in the country, at the Treasury, working out everybody's tax, and balance-of-payment trends, and God knows what. Now, you asked my harem out there something about a newspaper interview. That right?"

"Well, I wished to ask someone's advice. I met yesterday a journalist who also lives in Horseman's Yard..."

"Frank," interrupted Mr. Mann. "Yes, I've been talking to him. He's about top at his job, much less wild in print than he is in speech—you're just his sort of story. Do you want me to say yes or no?"

Humayan was put out, but tried not to show it. Of course he was delighted by the idea of an interview with a top journalist on a world-famous paper, but for professional reasons it was important that the interview should be thrust upon him and not sought out.

"I am indifferent," he said. "I wish to help the Glisters to remain on good terms with their neighbours. I do not wish to be a mystery man. But nor do I wish to impede my own work."

"Or the work of the Board?" said Mr. Mann, grinning.

"Of course, of course."

"Let's talk about your work for a minute. Are they treating you OK up there? Like your room? We can easily have you shifted."

"When my work goes well I am happy. When it goes badly I am miserable. It does not matter where I do it. Last Saturday afternoon, sitting at my bare table in my little room at Horseman's Yard and looking at a wall like that one, I made a useful breakthrough. I am not boasting. That is just an example. My work went well. I was happy."

"Tell me about that bit."

"Oh, it is a very technical piece of statistics."

"Try. Mind if I take a tape? I know a bit of statistics—

69

have to in my job—but I'll probably need to go through it several times."

Humayan explained in the simplest terms of which the material admitted. Mr. Mann followed him surprisingly far for a layman.

"Well, thanks for cutting out the jargon," he said as he clicked the recorder off. "A lot of boffins would have wrapped that up in clouds of verbiage. Not that you needed to—I doubt if I'll be able to sort it out however often I play that tape through. Where does it get us?"

"Its virtues are negative. Effectively it keeps us where we are, by preventing us from slipping back. As I study this problem I find it becomes increasingly complex; this piece of work allows me to treat what appeared to be a whole new group of unrelated variables as having mathematical links with a previous group of variables."

"But your original discovery still holds water?"

"Oh yes, of course. This is the usual way with scientific knowledge. There comes the flash—so!—like lightning in the collied night; for that instant you can see the landscape ahead, and it remains sharp on your retina after the flash is gone. But even so you, and the others who follow you, have to grope your way forward until there is another flash, seen probably by someone else. Newton saw such a flash. Einstein. I too, P. P. Humayan. Now I am groping, but I know in which direction to grope."

This was an almost word-for-word crib of his old Director's address to first-year research students—indeed Humayan had often wondered what a night looked like when it was collied.

"Fine," said Mr. Mann. "Now, I don't expect anybody's said this to you, Pete. We learn to be a flannel-mouthed bunch in this building, because we know anything we say is going to be picked up and chucked back at us by left-wing creeps, so we wrap it up nice and soft. You're really here to do two jobs: first there's the business of forecasting population trends—the Old Man spoke to you about that, I think, and it *is* important. But it's long-term. I mean, we'd like to know, but my guess is it might be twenty, thirty years before we run into another jump in the green chart—and by then we'll have people—the people who matter—conditioned to PNPC."

Humayan made a baffled noise.

"Post Natal Population Control," explained Mr. Mann. "But don't you worry about it, Pete—it'll probably never come to that. I know it sounds a nasty idea, but it's always been Nature's way, hasn't it? You've seen it back home?"

Humayan nodded, remembering the burning ghats.

"OK," said Mr. Mann. "Now all that side of it's important—forecasting trends, I mean—but it's not something I need to know *now*. What I really want from you, or from you and a few other guys, is a way of reaching accurate criteria of who is or isn't a Celt, regardless of the colour of their skins. In this country we've been spared the Cape Coloured problem they have in SA. We've got no mulattos. You're either white or green. At first that looked like a blessing, but it isn't, because why? Because it means we've got a lot of crypto-Celts walking around in white skins."

"But..."

"Wait a bit, Pete. I know what you're going to say. You're not a geneticist. I know you're not. But ultimately this is a statistical problem. When the Good Lord divides the sheep from the goats, he's not going to go messing around with each animal's life history. He'll know a goat when he sees one and he'll say, 'Right, you lot, stand over there.' That's what I want—a way of telling Celts from Saxons, in large batches, regardless of the colour of their skins. We don't want this to develop into a colour problem, do we?"

"I suppose not," said Humayan vaguely. His mind was already occupied with the problem that had been posed him. The Director had certainly spoken in the vaguest terms of the problem of forecasting population trends, but had implied (as Directors tend to) that Humayan's work here was to be pure science, knowledge for its own sake. Being a pragmatic fellow he had doubted this, but had not enquired further at the time; he knew quite well that fairly soon some quiet organiser would slip into the Laboratory to ask how his work was going and whether

71

his chair was comfortable, and at the same time tell him what his results were expected to be. That is the manner of research projects, only Mr. Mann's demands were going to be difficult to link in any way to the work he was actually doing, and intended to go on doing.

"There will be a lot of variables," he said.

"Sure, sure," said Mr. Mann, "but governments have their uses. You tell us where, and maybe we can fix some of those variables for you."

He prodded his index finger on to his desk, as if pinning a variable through its abdomen. Then he laughed.

"If this was a fascist country like Frank and the Doc make out, we could simply say it was a problem of racial purity, and start breeding back to pure strains—you've seen those stinking little dogs of his?"

"They are not much of a recommendation for the process of breeding back," said Humayan, surprised by Mr. Mann's knowledge of the Glister household and the animosity in his tone. Mr. Mann must have sensed the doubt.

"OK," he said, rising. "I'm very glad to have you pulling for us, Pete. You let me know as soon as you come up with anything I can use. And listen, anything you want—more data, ten thousand ear-measurements—and you can't get it through the Lab or on your budget, let me know. If you say it's got a bearing, I'll have men out on the streets measuring ears that very afternoon. OK?"

"Thank you," said Humayan gravely. It would be gratifying to be able to set this facility in motion, but at the moment he could think of no conceivable use for ear-measurements.

"You may think your work's academic," said Mr. Mann, moving towards the door with him. "But to us it's not, I tell you. We've got the situation all buttoned down, as of now—these bombs you hear, the odd kidnapping, that's just giving off steam. But if the pressure builds up much more, then pow! We'll have the Thames foaming with blood, just like old Enoc says. Doc Glister played you that record?"

"No, I don't think so," said Humayan automatically.

72

Half his mind was busy with aspects of the wholly impractical problem Mr. Mann had posed him, and the other half purring with gratification at the attentions shown to him by this important official. Only when the door was open and the hands reaching for each other did he remember what he had come for.

"This interview?" he said.

"That's OK," said Mr. Mann. "It's a free country, and you can talk to anyone you want, within reason, within reason. Just don't let the RRB down. If you say something a bit out of place, we can always put it right for you before it's printed, but it's easier not to have to. You'll find Frank's damned sharp, but he's got his heart in the right place—I think. So long, Pete. I've got a slab of work waiting, but we'll have another chat when things ease up."

Mr. Mann had clasped Humayan's hand at the beginning of this speech and held it to the end. He had a grip like iron.

Half-way through the morning his telephone rang. It was the official at India House, speaking in a very friendly fashion and saying that there was an answer to his telegram waiting for him. He walked round during the lunch hour and picked the message up. It said: "FIRST CLASS MANTRA AGAINST WITCHES IN PREPARATION STOP MEANWHILE ADVISED FOLLOWING FORMULA EFFICACIOUS QUOTE DA NARA DA GABA DEE END QUOTE REPEAT AS NECESSARY STOP YOUR EVER LOVING MOTHER."

Uncle Prim had had a hand in that. Efficacious was his favourite word, representing for him that unattainable Eden where gadgets worked and money-making schemes made money.

The rest of his lunch hour Humayan spent in the RRB library. The books on Ogham came from a locked case and were smudgy with use. He found it was an absurdly primitive script—you drew a horizontal line right across the page, and the first five letters were lines branching vertically up from this, one line for B, two for L, three for V and so on. The next five letters were a set of similar lines branching vertically down; the next five were slanting lines cutting right through the line; and the five vowels were vertical lines also cutting right through. Twenty clumsy letters, plus five even clumsier squiggles for seldom-used characters. So the mark on Mr. Leary's shoulder-blade was an H followed by a little cross, not in the alphabet, followed by either R or Ng (with this last letter the scars had run into each other, so it was difficult to tell whether there had been four lines or five). But as the central line was vertical, you could turn your head the other way and read the symbols differently—R or Ng, then the little cross, then B. It meant nothing to Humayan, other than being a menacing bit of mystery attached to the man who was going to interview him that evening.

At work that afternoon he paid very little attention to the goals at which he had been told to aim. He had early discovered that for a scientist to produce the results his masters desire it is no use his falsifying his processes; some other scientist will gladly publish a paper pointing out the error. Humayan had done this himself, in the past. The first essential is to discover the truth, because until you do that neither you nor your masters know where falsification can safely begin. So he worked in his usual way, steadily quartering the vast jungle-tracts of figures, with his Telex like some hound or shikari obedient at his side, but all the time with his mind alert for the crack of a betraying twig that would release him to plunge along the random trail of fleeing truth. That day he discovered nothing he did not already know; but towards evening, just as he began to crossfile his material on his own system that allowed him to use the memory-store of the big machine in the basement as two extra dimensions of interrelation, he began to be teased by the notion that if he went on for a few hours more a twig would snap. He sighed. He had this appointment with Kate's lover. Glenda would not be pleased if he missed that.

He sighed again as he locked the Telex rigid for the night, so that it could not be tampered with. All the machines in the building had locks, and locking them had been the only subject about which the Director had been less than vague during his interview with Humayan. All input and output devices must be locked when not in use.

Mr. Leary's living room was exactly the same shape as the Glisters' but totally different in feel. Its plush mess was dominated by a large poster taped to one wall, which showed a vivid green face, a priest's habit, and an arm with a green hand pointing straight at the viewer. Beside the figure was printed, "Your Church Needs You." Humayan, orange juice in hand, stared at this poster. It awoke vague memories.

"That is a recruiting slogan for the first war against Germany, I believe," he said.

"You misbelieve," said Mr. Leary, turning from the drinks-cupboard with a glass in his hand. "It's a steal from an English recruiting poster, but it's Irish, 1921. The English got right out of Ireland then, only too glad to go, now there was no money in agriculture, and left the Irish to fight it out among themselves, Prots in the north against Papists in the south. They're still at it. It's a bloody shambles, and that's how it's going to stay. They've achieved a balance of blood, killing each other off exactly as fast as they breed. You should see some of the stuff that comes on to our news-desk from Dublin— we don't use much of it because it's so bloody monotonous, but every so often we run a small story, just to remind readers that everything's a bit worse somewhere else. Cheers."

Still standing he sniffed disconsolately at his whisky, then drank it as if it were water. Humayan hovered, dubious where to settle. Mr. Leary seemed to own only one armchair, a thing like a shapeless bale, as though an explorer had discovered a mammoth frozen into a glacier, had cut it into sections and packed them in old chintz to ship home, and one section had arrived in this room to add its ambiances to all the male-smelling clutter.

"No, don't sit down," said Mr. Leary, whacking his rummer on a bookshelf. "I'm not going to wait for this bloody photographer any longer—I'll get a pic of you somehow. What I want to do is stroll up to the Green

Zone for a bit of local colour—I listen better on the hoof, too. OK?"

"I have an RRB pass now. Mr. Mann gave it to me."

"Dick? Boy, did you go to the top? What did he say about the interview?"

"He was pleased with the idea. I thought you would know from telephoning him."

"I forgot. Sorry. Overslept, you know."

The battered face smiled with sudden vehemence, as though all future happiness depended on Humayan both believing Mr. Leary and forgiving him. What if Mr. Mann himself had said the opposite? Humayan respected a certain secretiveness, and washed by that smile it was easy to ignore the lie, even for one who knew just what form Mr. Leary's oversleeping took.

After a week in England Humayan had still not become used to the lingering brightness of northern evenings; he felt that dusk by now ought to have been seeping its brown tones into the shadows, and was shocked to see the lobelias in the yard still as garish a blue as they had been at noon.

In the alley beside the inn they met a green postman carrying a moderate-sized but obviously heavy parcel.

"That for me?" said Mr. Leary.

"It is, sorr," said the postman.

"Great. I've been waiting for that. Hang on a second, Pete; it's some books I need."

The postman rolled his eyes to heaven as if shocked by the notion that anyone should actually need books. Mr. Leary took the parcel from him and went back into the Yard. Humayan followed the postman out on to the pavement and watched him adjust his bicycle clips and ride away on a ramshackle old delivery bicycle. His cap was too large for him and he had to cycle with one hand holding it to his scalp. Mr. Leary took a few minutes to reappear, but made no apology.

They walked together towards the Green Zone. Their paces did not match, but subconsciously both tried to adapt to the other's, Humayan stretching towards Mr. Leary's natural lope, and Mr. Leary contracting to a

76

mincing gait which assorted ill with his coarse muscularity. At first it was a very silent interview, with Mr. Leary simply humming and thinking. In the subway that divided Zone from Zone the mysterious slogan had been painted out, but a new one splashed in over the obliterating paint.

"Ogham," said Mr. Leary.

"Yes, I know. I can read the letters but not the language."

"Can you just? When did you learn that?"

"Oh, ah, I saw two youths painting a slogan and I was inquisitive, so I read it up in the RRB library. It is a very easy alphabet to learn; I read it through and I knew it."

"Well, if I were you I'd unlearn it. In a society like ours you find the cops are just as much prey to fashion as novelists or well-dressed women—they take it into their heads to crack down on this or that bit of Celticry on no rational grounds. Probably somebody wrote a slogan on some senior cop's garage doors, and it all began there. Anyway, they're very hot on it just now, so ... Hell, we'd better get on with the job—let's start with your work in India."

His questions were shrewd and coherent, but superficial. He seemed to have no interest in the inwardness of things. But he was a good listener and seldom failed to follow a train of argument. From time to time he would stop, lean his note-pad against a peeling wall and write down a key phrase. Humayan noticed while he was doing this that his hands had the same bashed-about appearance as his face; none of the fingers lay really parallel and the top joint of his left index finger was bent almost at right-angles to the rest of it. He took a path that led through a very drear district, not such as Humayan would have chosen to wander in, though the houses, when you looked at them, turned out to have much the same basic architecture as the spruce Victorian residences round Horseman's Yard. Once there had been here, too, neat plaster mouldings along cornices and over pillared porticoes, but these had long fallen away. Whole façades were black with the smoke of sea-coal; most windows were broken, and woodwork paintless; occasional houses were better preserved, but painted such curious colours that Humayan guessed the paint must have been a cheap job-lot, or stolen by workmen at some building-site. But the weighty architecture, the decay, gave most of the houses the look of those crumbling mausoleums in the British cemetery in Bombay.

The evening was full of the sweet, damp reek of un-collected garbage; dirt-smeared small children played unfathomable games along the pavements, glanced up with a flicker of eyes at the sound of footsteps, stared, then returned to their mysteries. A few green men lounged around in twos and threes. At one point a man came walking along the pavement towards them with his fawn shirt all covered with blood, and his nose cut and swollen.

"Are ye daein' weel, Jock?" shouted a man in a door-way.

The bleeding man stopped and pouted his crimson chest.

" 'Tis nae coward blude," he called. " 'Tis nae coward blude."

The man in the doorway answered indecipherably, and the bleeding man turned and stumped on with the sturdy, straddled gait of the confident drunk; but every ten yards he stopped and shouted back to the man in the doorway, " 'Tis nae coward blude." Increasing distance gave his call a more and more questioning tone, as though the original axiom was becoming dubious.

Humayan began to feel that they were never out of earshot of a crying baby. Unlit basement windows flickered bluely with TV. Silent women leaned from up-stairs windows. All the police were green, armed, paired and stolid; but Mr. Leary knew them all by their first names so Humayan never had to produce his pass. Their pale eyes swept over him without one gleam of interest.

He was careful, in telling his story, to riddle it with technicalities, some of which Mr. Leary wrote down. This was partly to impress the reporter with his intellectual stature, but mainly to make his actual work seem im-portant but impossible for a layman to follow. He did

78

not intend to make again the mistake he had made with Kate, claiming an achievement both large and simple. Mr. Leary seldom tried to clarify these obfuscations; his main interest was in likely practical results, and he was impatient of the notion that until you understood the cause you could not expect to predict the effects. After a while he switched ground, and began to try to turn the whole interview into a human-interest story. The change came at a point when Humayan was talking about a self-multiplying aberration common to the absorption curves of exiled populations of moderate sizes. Mr. Leary grunted and waved a battered hand at the townscape.

"You've seen this sort of thing in India, I suppose," he said.

They had come to a point where an elevated throughway moved in scooped and cantilevered arches above the roof-lines and then flowered into the great concrete petals of an interchange. Below this was a cleared space, vaguely grassed, where stood three smashed saplings and a children's climbing-frame, uprooted, on its side. In the light breeze bits of paper flopped a few feet, lay still, flopped on; the supply was endless. The sun had set now, and the spies of darkness were gathering under the arches; in one such shadow half-a-dozen fourteen-year-old boys had cornered a couple of girls; the jeering note of the backchat modulated a stage, the boys' voices becoming more confident, more eager, the girls' more irritably resigned. Two passing policemen took no notice; around the arena the dark houses had their backs turned on the scene, showing bustles of shambling huts and outside lavatories, and roofs patched with old doors and corrugated iron. Overhead the sleek traffic hustled to cosier zones.

"Oh, we have miles of cities much worse than this," said Humayan airily. "It is a pity, but nothing can be done. These people here do not know how lucky they are."

An electric tocsin clamoured under the arches and drowned Mr. Leary's answer. It rang for half a minute, and as it ceased one of the policemen turned and shrilled his whistle and shouted to the boys, who broke like

79

startled birds and ran away down alleys. The two girls, only a little dishevelled, walked across the grass gossiping angrily.

"Saved by the bell," said Mr. Leary.

"What happened?"

"Ten-minute warning for curfew. There's another in five minutes, and then the real thing. After that, if you meet a cop who feels like target practice ... oh, you'd be all right, with your pass, provided he gave you time to show it. Let's go. I've got all I want, but it's going to be a hell of a story to lick into shape."

Humayan scuttered beside him as he strode rapidly back through the dismal streets; they were still in the Zone when the real bell sounded, but the policemen they met after that answered Mr. Leary's "Good night" with a casual grumble. Humayan assumed that the journalist had exaggerated the dangers. It was what he would have done himself. Not far inside the Saxon Zone they came to a railed playground, with elaborate edifices for climbing and swinging, and a sandpit. Mr. Leary stopped here, though the gate was locked, and contemplated the sculpture-like shapes.

"We are living in the last days of the world," he said suddenly.

"I think the world has seen many last days," said Humayan. "You are lucky on this island, a rich, easy people. Your nightmares are things which other races take for granted. When they begin to become a little real, you think it is the end of the world."

Mr. Leary made an impatient gesture, then looked at his watch as though the end of the world was late.

"How may famines have you seen?" said Humayan.

"That's not the point," muttered Mr. Leary, but seemed not to wish to argue what the point *was*. They stood in silence looking at the empty playground. Slowly, as if had been waiting its cue, the dimming air trembled with a slow, deep thud, like an earthquake whose shock wave has travelled through the air.

"Hell, that was a big one!" said Mr. Leary. "They'll have to let me report that. But do you know what the News Editor will say? 'Play it down, Frank, old boy.

Play it down.' Come on. I've got to go and phone the office."

Glenda was lying on Humayan's bed, bespectacled, reading a school *Hamlet*. He was still feeling important, a man of consequence, and was irritated to see her thus in possession.

"Da Nara Da Gaba Dee," he mouthed.

"It's all right, I'm just going," she said, shutting her book.

It worked! It worked! He began to fiddle with the buckle of the little collar. She took off her spectacles, as if weary of the feel of them on her face, and looked at him. Looked into his middle eye.

"What did you find out about Frank?" she asked.

"Not very much. A senior official in the RRB says his heart is in the right place. The mark on his shoulders is Ogham. One of the letters is H or B, and the other is R or Ng. He thinks we are living in the last days of the world. It seems to me that at some time in his life he must have been tortured, and then branded. Perhaps more than once. A big parcel came for him just as we left for our walk. The postman..."

"Postman! At half past six!"

"Yes, and his bicycle was not of official pattern, I think, and his hat was much too big for him."

"What on earth? *Drugs*, Pete?"

"Far too big. I thought perhaps illegal pamphlets."

"If we could find out ... Anyway, I've had a foul day. I was kept in late for sacrificing cockroaches to the Great Minus One. We were going to dissect them anyway, so I couldn't see any harm in sacrificing them first, but Miss Frankins wouldn't see it. Helen was sick. What are you going to do now?"

"I am going to visit my friend Mr. Palati's restaurant and eat a very hot curry."

"Oh. All right. Enjoy yourself."

She moved out of the room with her curious clumsy glide. He locked the door and stood for a moment considering. The charm had worked, for a moment, but then she had overcome it by exerting her full powers. Still there was virtue in the charm, however weak; perhaps in her absence it would counteract the power of the dog-collar. He undid the buckle and settled down at the table to write the words along the inner surface of the leather.

The collar had an ornamental line of stitching running between the brass nodules; this went right through the leather, forming a single horizontal line along the centre of the reverse side. He stared at it. This too was meant, planned from the beginning by his protecting planets. His hands shook as he unzipped the compartment at the back of his wallet and drew out the carbon copy of his horoscope that he kept there, two flimsy sheets of typescript brown with much fingering and worn at the folds almost to the point where they fluttered into separate rectangles. "... to travel into far lands ... To be troubled with a witch. To face dangers. To acquire new wisdoms from old sages, and by these to overcome the dangers..."

It didn't say anything about overcoming the witch, but she seemed to be linked with the dangers. The old sages were of course the ancient druids. Using the line of stitching as his central mark, he wrote the charm along the leather, using Ogham characters. Naturally the charm would be more efficacious in that form. He buckled the collar back on and went out.

"Oho, yes," said Mr. Palati, grinning like one of Hanuman's apes. "I am sure there are such places. One moment, one moment only, and I will telephone. No, no, my friend, every man to his tastes and needs. Did not Brahma make all men different? Oh, I know a fellow, an Egyptian I tell you, who can only enjoy himself at the top of a step-ladder. Yes, I tell you, and it was worse than that. He is one of those fellows who wants a different lady each time. I have seen him bicycling round Hammersmith with his ladder—he pretends to be a window-cleaner, you know? The girls all call him Pharaoh, and he is bicycling round all the houses looking for fresh girls who do not have vertigo. I am a joking man, so I tell him he must take out an insurance policy, to insure the girls for industrial accidents, you know. Poor Pharaoh, he did not understand that I am making a joke, and he does what I tell him, but he was not lucky with his broker, who telephones the Home Office, very English, you know, and so poor Pharaoh is deported. Oh, easy, they follow him and catch him with a green girl. But at Ramadan he sent me a postcard of the pyramids, saying now he is married and very happy. No, no, I know what you are thinking. You are a naughty fellow, like me!"

Selina was unpredictably large, and the shower-room was small. She frowned as she dried, towelling her back like an athlete so that her big breasts lolloped to and fro, tracing and retracing the graph-curve of an erotic equation. Humayan dried in the corner away from the shower, dodging her vigorous arms.

"I thought you'd know how to do it," she said. "I mean blokes with funny ideas usually do."

"Ladies in India are not so tall."

"Still, we managed in the end, didn't we. It's a bit of a change, something like that, I always say, and a change is as good as a rest if you see what I mean."

"In certain cases I agree," said Humayan. He was tired.

"Listen to you! D'you mind if I ask you something a bit personal, Pete?"

"The reason for my perversion is that a witch has put a spell on me."

"Is that true? Really, that's thrilling! I must tell Marge and I promise it won't go no further. She's as secret as the grave—she has to be. She's in charge of all the cleaning, see, at the Race Relations. She's my sister, and we've always told each other all our secrets, so that's how I know it won't go no further. I mean, she'd be in dead trouble if they found out at the Relations what I do for a living—such a puritan lot you never!"

Humayan made a small sound of protest but she gabbled on unheeding.

"Anyway it wasn't that I wanted to ask, Pete. I mean that really *is* personal—I wouldn't ask something like that —not first time, anyway. No ... well, I mean, you know,

83

well it's actually the first time I've gone with a coloured bloke, and I don't mind telling you my first idea was at least in a shower I'll know he's clean, if you see what I mean. I mean there's no way of telling, is there? You aren't offended, are you? And then I thought, well, really it's not any different from white blokes, except you're a bit cleverer than some, once we worked out how, and kept it up a bit longer. Honestly, some of these boys, it makes me wonder what they think they're spending their money on. They might be on piece-work, I tell Marge. No, what I wondered was if *you* think there's any difference, apart from everybody being a bit different anyway, if you know what I mean."

This is a poser, thought Humayan as he eased himself into a shirt that despite the shower-curtain their activities had somehow dampened. Next time he would bring a large plastic bag. Having so far kept the deception up he did not want to admit that he had never before made love in a shower-bath—which despite initial problems had produced a pleasingly invigorating effect and helped him not to disgrace his country by an inadequate performance. And, besides the novelty of the sluicing water, there was the fact that you could have carved two Indian girls out of Selina and still had meat to spare. He thought back to Penelope, a white woman who worked in a Bombay brothel and despite a certain scrawniness was able to charge extra because of the colour of her skin though another girl had once told Humayan that Penelope was really only a rather pale half-caste. As a statistical sample Penelope was both small and suspect, but she would have to do.

"There is a little difference in the texture of the skin," he said judiciously, "but nothing essential varies."

"Listen to you!" she crowed. "Nothing essential! Marge will love that—she's got a lovely sense of humour. But it was all right, wasn't it?"

"Very nice," said Humayan, interested that despite the day-in, day-out nature of her trade she was still animated by a sexual patriotism similar to his own. "Indian ladies are very nice too, of course."

"It's a funny thing," she said, moving her towel to the

84

steppe-land of her thighs and thus allowing him space to wriggle into his trousers, "it's a funny thing but sometimes you get a bloke in here who won't talk about anything except all the Greenies he's had, and what a wonderful screw they were. But we had a girl in here once, a funny kind of girl, very nice spoken, and I don't know what happened but suddenly she come all over liberal and went off to work in a house near the docks where you get all kinds of things happening and the cops look the other way. It was against her principles to work in a racialist house, you see. And she come in here six months later and we had a bit of a chat and she said she wasn't suffering for her principles at all, and she'd met a Chinaman she wanted to marry only he wanted a yellow wife. Anyway, she's a nun now. But I'm not like that at all, not me. I've never told anyone this except Marge, but I get a nightmare, over and over again, and it's the whole Welsh rugby team come in after Twickenham, all wanting me and all smelling of leeks. And when I wake up I know it's only a dream, and I know that they don't come to Twickenham any more, and they wouldn't be allowed in here not in the last six years, but I'm still ever so frightened."

"I did not realise that the miscegenation laws were so recent."

"Lordy, yes. All these freedom movements, equality and such, that's quite a modern thing. My grannie kept a house in Cheltenham—we've come down in the world a bit, but she owned the freehold, she did, and she told me —she's dead now, of course—she told me Royalty used to look in when they was in that part of the world with no bridges to open special, only she was such a snob I doubt if it happened more than once. But she did tell me that in her day, in a nice area like that—it was different in places like ports of course—in a nice area like that you didn't have to have no laws, because the Greenies knew their place and, well, they all knew what would have happened to a green boy what showed his face in a white house. But then of course the Greenies started getting ideas and there was clergymen and communists taking their side—though seeing some of the clergymen we get in here I can't think how anyone paid any attention to *them*—and so of course we had to start having laws, just to keep things decent."

"I see," said Humayan, taking his wallet out of his jacket.

"You pay Mrs. Cholmondely, down in the foyer," said Selina. "Unless you've got a Diner's Card, that is."

"I understand," said Humayan, "but I would like to give you a little present too."

He put two clean pound notes down on a miraculously dry segment of the bathroom stool, and immediately wondered whether one would have been enough.

"That's ever so kind of you," said Selina earnestly. "Will you be coming back then?"

"I hope so."

"That's nice. Just give Mrs. Cholmondely a tinkle and I'll make sure the bathroom's free."

Next morning he found on his desk a column of paper which had not been there the night before. Automatically he read the line of figures and letters at the top and tried to relate them to his work; then he realised that they were printing instructions and read on:

"Pete Humayan does not look as though he could change the world. He is slight and large-eyed. He stares at England with a look of polite but withdrawn reserve. He landed in England only one week ago, but already the people who matter are beginning to know that Pete Humayan could change the world. Your world. My world."

Really, these layman, thought Humayan, beginning to purr as he read. Mr. Leary—or rather Frank Lear, for that was how the article was signed—had written a very friendly piece, and had even got most of the facts he quoted approximately right. The exaggerations seemed to Humayan most pardonable. It was unfortunate that the main scientific bias of the article concentrated on the possibility of forecasting the birth of green children to white parents—a phenomenon which at the moment was statistically negligible, but around which, it was clear, a considerable body of popular myth had accumulated. The background of their previous night's stroll was splashed on with thick paint "...while around us the life of a Celtic Zone unwound its skein of misery ...at last the clamour of curfew pierced the ugly dusk..." The concluding paragraph contrasted the locked and tidy playground in the White Zone with the uprooted climbing-frame under the through-way loop, and the judder of that bomb: "How soon will this noise become the only language that race speaks to race? Can Pete Humayan do anything to prevent that day coming?"

The telephone rang as he was reading that sentence second time through and thinking what a lot of fuss they were making about their problems: 2,197 deaths last year, enough for one moderate-sized Madras riot ...

"Humayan," he said in the brisk voice of a man who could change the world.

"Hi, Pete. This is Dick Mann. You read that piece of Frank's."

"Yes, yes indeed. I have just finished. I am afraid it's very sensational."

"Come off it! You couldn't ask for a better ad, and nor could we. But has he got his facts right?"

"I think so, but the emphasis..."

"Bugger the emphasis. Nothing you want changed?"

"No, er, bearing in mind that it is popular journalism..."

"Popular with you, anyway. He's come the Wordsworths a bit strong at the end—that type always feel they've got to pull out the organ-stops. It'll be a kindness to tell him to lop a bit out here and there. Tighten it up. It'll be interesting to see how many of the others bite. So long."

At first Humayan was distracted from his work by a tendency to re-read bits of Mr. Leary's article, but after an hour he folded it and put it in a drawer. He toiled steadily along dull paths for two more hours, but just before lunch, when his mouth and stomach were already forecasting their own pleasure with sweet juices, the beast of insight stirred amid the thickets. He scribbled a 'Do not disturb' notice, taped it to his door, turned the key in the lock and settled by the printer. His mind left his body to nose along the intricate tracks. Even the clack and chicker of the print-out and the lines of lit figures jerking into being on the Telex became remote to his numb senses, though it was he who caused them. These things were for the moment extensions of himself, functioning unnoticed, as did his lungs and heart. The big computer in the basement performed its miracles as if it were a limb of his own mind.

Five hours later all his muscles shuddered as the soul came back to sit behind the pineal nerve. He filled half a page of paper with handwritten symbols, clipped to it the three sheets of print-out that showed the true track, kicked into one corner the mound of doublings and false trails, and began to massage the tensions out of his left fingers which had been hovering all that time above the keys.

V

THE MINISTER FOR INTERNAL DEFENCE (Sir Lorimer Proudfoot)—As Hon. Members are aware, these shocking explosions are the work of an irresponsible minority—
MRS. STRAUSS (Hampstead: Independent Liberal)— These bombs express the frustrations of the whole Celtic Nation. (Shouts of "No. No!")
SIR LORIMER—If the Hon. Member for Hampstead is right, then the whole Celtic Nation is an irresponsible minority.
HON. MEMBERS—Hear, Hear! (Laughter.)

When Humayan came back to Horseman's Yard he was confoundedly hungry, but too tired to go out to Mr. Palati's, or even to open a tin and warm up its contents; so he was delighted to find on the carpet outside his door a square white box containing a clumsily iced cake. The icing was pink, and green letters spelt out the word PEECE.

Much relieved that the ridiculous feud with Moirag appeared to be over, and salivating at the thought of all that sticky sweetness for himself alone, he unlocked his door and put the cake on the table. While he washed his hands the collar on his left wrist became itchy, and continued to be so as he fetched a knife and plate from the kitchen. He was fidgeting irritably with it when someone knocked softly at the door. He called out. Glenda crept in, grinning.

"Hello," she said. "You look dead beat."

"I am tired, yes, but I am happy. I did good work this afternoon and now Moirag has forgiven me and made me a cake."

"No! Let's have a look! God, it looks absolutely poisonous!"

"Do you think so?" said Humayan in a shocked whisper.

"What? Oh, *poisonous*? No, of course not. Well, I mean, I shouldn't think so, but you never know with Greens. I mean, I suppose you did have a row with her, and you're living in her room—at least she thinks it's her room still—and ... oh, I'm sure it's all right."

Humayan stared at the cake. It looked much less succulent now. The collar on his wrist had stopped itching.

"Anyway," said Glenda, "where would she get the poison? We could try it on the dogs, I suppose, but they'd probably be sick anyway. I know what, let's go out to the park and feed it to the pigeons and see what happens. Only ... have you got anything else to eat? Good-oh, here's a tin of chicken breast. I'll nick some bread and make a couple of sandwiches—it's ages till supper. She's taken the dogs for a walk, so if we go now ..."

In the park, behind low wooden palings, a number of birds strutted and mooched. The larger ones were exotic, peacocks and bantams and gold pheasants, but between these incredible promontories of colour the grass festered with sooty pigeons. Two yellowish tots were crumbling bread between the palings, watched by a green nanny in brown uniform, watched in turn by two square-shouldered men. Humayan had brought only one slice of the cake in a paper bag, at the rustle of which a splinter-group of birds moved in his direction.

"Not the pigeons," said Glenda. "They might fly away. Try that peacock."

It wasn't easy. The pigeons were nippy and the peacock stately and bored until a peahen came up, drab and meek and greedy. The peacock lost interest in food, shook himself with an irritable rattle of plumes and, as if involuntarily, began the slow erection of his tail-feathers. Humayan watched this process with a remote but genuine thrill of sympathy for the poor beast's enormous, unavailing beauty and dignity; for the peahen, as if in deliberate rebuff, pecked about among the pigeons and paid no attention either to the iridescent sail of plumes, or to the soft buff-coloured underpants revealed when the male's dance brought him backside-on to her, or to the shivering rattle of the quills.

"You're missing her," said Glenda. "For heaven's sake look what you're doing."

Humayan crumbled and tossed with great attention until the cake was gone.

"Let's go and sit down," she said. "We can see what happens from over there. How long shall we give it?"

"Ten minutes. This is all very foolish."

"I'm enjoying myself. Here's your sandwich. I wonder whether there's anything in the by-laws about poisoning pigeons—you'd better say it's part of your religion if anyone makes a fuss. I'm sure it's part of mine—it's just the kind of thing old Minus One fancies. Who do you think those men are? They don't look as if they were here for fun. Oh, I know, those brats must belong to some ambassador—Spanish I should think—and everyone's got into such a kerfuffle over this other old geezer that they've all got bodyguards in case ... Crikey!"

Her exclamation was almost drowned by a weird noise from the enclosure. The peahen had embarked on a staggering parody of the cock's dance; her beak was raised to the sky and emitted in staccato bursts the agonising wail of the species; this uproar was enough to alarm the pigeons who whirled away with clapping wings, so that when the peahen stopped her performance and keeled over on her side it was possible to see that five or six sooty grey bodies were already lying inert on the grass. For a while the peacock continued his display, too self-absorbed to notice that his inamorata was no more; but the two bodyguards frowned, glanced round among the tree-trunks and slid their hands into their coat pockets.

"Golly!" said Glenda. "Let's be off!"

"That will only make things worse," said Humayan, putting his hand into his jacket and withdrawing his wallet; he saw the larger bodyguard's hand begin to snatch something from the pocket, and then relax as the wallet came into view. The man strode towards him, still wary, as Humayan withdrew the orange RRB pass. The hard but unhealthy features did not change, but the man flicked into view a rather similar piece of blue pasteboard, then put it away and took Humayan's pass. He studied the photograph, stared at Humayan with opaque eyes, withdrew a little notebook from another pocket and wrote down some details from the pass, which he handed back.

"Thank you, sir," he said.

After a shrugging colloquy with his mate they whistled to the nanny and jerked their heads. One of the children had managed to reach the corpse of a pigeon and was trying to pull it through the palings. The nanny snatched both children away. They were crying as she led them down the path. The watchers followed, heavy-footed.

Before Humayan could act in any way to release his inner tension a park-attendant came up the path pushing a barrow with gardening tools in it. This man, bearded and green-faced, halted by the enclosure and scratched his head, miming astonishment, when he saw the dead birds. He stepped over the paling and threw the pigeons' bodies into a clump of bamboo, but when he picked up the peahen he hefted it thoughtfully by the legs, glanced round, and quickly slid the body under a piece of sacking in his barrow. At last he trundled away.

"Golly!" said Glenda. "There must have been enough in there to poison the whole school!"

"I will not stand for it!" hissed Humayan. "It is intolerable!"

"Being poisoned, you mean? But you weren't."

"I shall go now to the police!"

"No! No! You can't do that! Then it might all come out about Kate and that creep Frank. Besides Mum's very fond of Moirag. No, Pete, you can't! I won't let you!"

Shiveringly Humayan ran his fingers round the brass knobs of the collar. Furious with fear though he was, he knew he would have to obey. And after all, she had saved him; even before she came into the room and spoke the saving word, the collar had tried to protect him. So this was evidence that she was a very powerful witch indeed, though he suspected that she was still too young to have any real idea of her own powers; it would be most unsafe to thwart her over a matter like this.

"Most unsafe," he muttered.

"Oh, she won't try it again. They're real bird-brains, you know—they never carry anything through. I tell you what—Moirag's frightfully superstitious; we'll go home and you can thank her for the cake and tell her how good it was and she'll think that Indians can eat poison without being ill. I wish I knew where she got it."

"It does not matter. I will move. I will go to an hotel. I cannot stay in your house if people keep trying to poison me."

"Oh no! You can't go! Life's so much more interesting now I've got you!"

Another order. Humayan shrugged and walked with her down the slant path under the lime-trees, past the adventure playground to the park gates. Perhaps Glenda's plan was a good one, he thought. It would produce a strong reaction from Moirag, who was too simple a creature to control her emotions; that would betray her guilt, and then he would be able to consult Doctor Glister about the proper course of action. He would not tell Glenda that he was going to consult her father, or she would forbid it. Yes, that was the sensible, mature, course of action. Humayan thought that any man could be forgiven a certain emotionalism in such circumstances, but the responsible citizen considers his duty to himself and to society, chooses the proper path, and firmly bids the monsters of shock and horror back into their dens.

Unfortunately Moirag was loitering at the gates into Horseman's Yard when they returned. The two little dogs were deciding where they could most inconveniently excrete.

"It's a grand evening, Miss Anne," she said. "And I have baked a cake for you, Mister."

Her bland, slurred voice, her unreadable pale eyes, her

unpractised smile, all twisted Humayan's guts. The monsters surged back, yelping, into the open.

"I have seen your cake," he hissed. "I have fed it to the birds! They fell down dead!"

"Pete! Pete!" cried Glenda.

"You were feeding my cake to the birds?" said Moirag.

"Yes, for you are trying to poison me. I have witnesses. And you filled my orange juice with salt! I will not permit it!"

"A gentleman would not be making his complaints in the open road," said Moirag. She was still smiling and her eyes glittered. A window or two opened round the upper storey of the Yard.

"Yes, I know you!" shouted Humayan. "You are a wicked woman! You want to kill me. You want to kill me because I know your wickedness! Yes!"

"Do stop it, Pete," said Glenda.

"Ach, don't be fashed, Miss Anne," said Moirag. "The little blackamoor's been drinking, surely. He does not look to me to have a gey strong head on him."

Humayan's tongue forgot his English and he cursed her in shrilling Hindustani until a strong hand gripped his elbow.

"What the hell's up?" said Mr. Leary.

"Moirag's been a bit silly," said Glenda. "She's been teasing Pete, and it's upset him."

"So I should bloody well think," said Mr. Leary. "Go away, Moirag. You're a stupid old bag, and you ought to know better than trying to come it over a visitor to this isle of ours; tsk tsk. Now come along, old fellow. Don't take it too hard. What's all this about wickedness?"

"Nothing. Nothing," muttered Humayan. He was weak and ashamed, as though his rage had been like the vomit which the little dog had spewed over Horseman's Yard's trim paving—and that had been no more the dog's fault than this was his.

"Nothing," he said again. Moirag smiled and looked sideways at Mr. Leary, who stared thoughtfully back at her, rubbing his bearded chin.

"You'll be late for curfew," said Glenda, placidly.

Moirag opened her mouth, shut it again, nodded and

lurched off. Mr. Leary relaxed his grip on Humayan's arm.

"Come along, Pete," he said again. "This sort of thing's hell, I know, but you never get anywhere by reacting. The only hope is to pay no attention and then they get to realise that it won't wash. Come and have a stiff noggin of ... oh, you don't. Sorry, old fellow, I forgot. But you can't expect Moirag to know a thing like that."

This too was intolerable. The Poona voice, put on to express the false sympathy. Mr. Leary had clearly heard, and enjoyed, a lot of the quarrel before he had chosen to intervene. He was a cruel man. Humayan turned and rushed for the door of Number Six.

"Nothing, nothing," he muttered to the one-man committee of Glisters who stood waiting in the hallway.

"I'll explain," said Glenda.

He scuttered miserably upstairs to lie on his bed and contemplate a future diet taken solely from unopened tins. Compounding his misery was the knowledge that after this it would be quite impossible to do any real work tomorrow.

Work proved impossible in any case. First there was an intrusive paper on his desk again, a proper newspaper open at a spread which started in enormous letters with the words "WILL *YOU* HAVE A GREEN BABY? HE KNOWS." The photograph was the same as the one on his pass, but showing more background. A broad white arrow had been cut from it, to join the screaming type to his own head. The article had been much condensed from the version he had read yesterday. Many pleasing references to himself had been omitted, besides a number of comments on the bleaker aspects of life in a Green Zone. The scientific basis was now seriously distorted. The final impression was that this funny little brown man had been imported by the RRB to work a single rapid miracle, allay one central anxiety in the Saxon soul, and then be politely exported again. The telephone rang.

"Dick Mann here."

"I have read it."

"What? Oh yes, that. Came out quite well in the end."

"It is very unbalanced in my opinion."

"No harm in that. Bit of a smoke-screen about what you're really here for, Pete. It's stirring up a lot of interest already, and I want to talk to you about that. But there's another thing, more urgent ... Can you nip down and have a word with me? Fine. Stay there and Tarquin will come and collect you. Couple of minutes."

Humayan took yesterday's version from the drawer and compared it with today's. The maddening thing was that there was no single sentence about which he could complain without seeming a self-centred prima donna. But it was no use to his career now, no use at all.

Tarquin turned out to be the young man whom he had previously seen in Mr. Mann's outer office placing bets on horse races.

"It is kind of you to come," said Humayan, "but I think I could have found my own way."

"There are ways and ways," said Tarquin with a play-boy's laugh and led him out of the laboratory to a fire-cupboard; he opened the door and twisted the reel of the fire-hose, exposing a keyhole into which he inserted an instrument like a miniature ice-pick. He turned it and pushed; the back of the cupboard swung in so that they could enter a narrow bleak chamber with a lift-shaft in one side. The lift took them down to another such chamber, whence they emerged through another fire-cupboard into Tarquin's office.

Nothing had changed about Mr. Mann's room, but Mr. Mann looked larger and bleaker as he slid a sheet of purple typing across the desk.

"What in hell's name have you been up to?" he said.

Humayan's hands shook, which made the symbols difficult to read, but he made out the top line of figures which showed him that this was a report from some security district which had been processed by the central computer and because it referred to him had been channelled to Mr. Mann's desk. His confident reading of the various codes steadied him. He was beginning to know that computer pretty well.

The message said: "DUTY 9958/16/23G. DAY-LOG 7. 83831 SGT COWKER. EXTRACT. 1941 HRS. WITH KIDS IN HD

PK. NURSE MCNABB (CHK LVL 8). KIDS FED BIRDS. TWO PERSONS (M BROWN, FW) APPROACHED TO FEED BIRDS CARRYING ONE SLICE FRESH CAKE IN PAPER BAG. APPEARED MORE EXCITABLE THAN NORMAL ADULT BIRD CRANKS. FINISHED CAKE. RETIRED TO BENCH AND TALKED IN LOW VOICES. DISCUSSED SELF AND OFFICER FROST. AT 1957 HRS LARGE BIRD SQUAWKED AND DROPPED DEAD. BODY COUNT ALSO SEVEN PIGEONS (ESTIMATE). ON MY APPROACH W F WISHED TO RUN BUT BROWN M PRODUCED RRB PASS. DETAILS AS FOLLOWS . . ."

Humayan knew the details by heart so he didn't bother to read them. "Yes," he said in a meditative voice.

"What the hell do you mean 'Yes'? We didn't ship you over here to poison pigeons—and what was that other thing—a goose?"

"A peahen. By 'Yes' I mean that it must have appeared odd and I am very glad of this opportunity to discuss it with you."

"Sit down. Fire ahead."

"The Glisters employ a maid called Moirag McSomething . . ."

Mr. Mann's stubby fingers hovered a moment above the keys of his Telex, then moved with expert speed.

". . . and a stupid feud developed between us because she wished to clean my room and I prefer to do so myself. It used to be her room, you see, before the new zoning laws. We have had one argument, and she has made little attempts to persecute me, such as bringing me a drink full of salt at the Sunday morning party in Horseman's Yard."

"What do you make of all that?" said Mr. Mann.

"Oh, they seem very nice people. Very friendly."

"They are the necessary hypocrites," said Mr. Mann with quiet vehemence. "You've got to have them in a country like ours—people who know which side their bread is buttered but who're prepared to make a little song and dance if the machinery for keeping them comfortable starts playing a bit rough with the Greens. They make me . . . sorry, Pete, carry on."

"Well, when I got home last night she had left a cake for me, iced, with the word 'Peace' on it. I thought that was nice of her and I was just going to eat some when

97

Miss Glenda came in and said, by way of a jest, that it looked poisonous. And then, you know, I thought this was funny, Moirag making up the feud like that. She is not the type. But I am a cautious man so Miss Glenda and I took a slice to the park and fed it to the birds. It was fortunate we did so."

"Too bloody right. You tell Doc Glister? Local police? Nothing's come through except this."

He tapped the report.

"I was very upset, and Miss Glenda wished me to pretend to Moirag that I had eaten the cake. She has a malicious sense of humour, you see. Also the Glisters are kind hosts, and Miss Glenda said she would explain to her father. I do not know what she told him, but he said nothing when I met him this morning. I was intending to tackle him tonight."

"You've got the rest of the cake?"

"I am sorry. I was most upset. I cut it in small pieces and flushed it down the lavatory."

"Hell. Then..."

The machine beside the Telex clicked, fizzed and shot a rectangle of card across the desk. Mr. Mann glanced at it and passed it over. The photograph was a good likeness, in colour, the green very vivid. Moirag McBain, alias Smith, and a few lines of coded symbols. Mr. Mann took it back and studied it for a while.

"See what happened to the birds?" he said suddenly.

Humayan told him. He got up and fetched a large-scale map of London from a bookshelf and made him point out the exact spot where they had fed the birds. Then he lifted one of his telephones.

"Tarquin? Good. No, not half done yet, you'll have to stave them off another half hour. Now, lad, here's a few chores. Get a man out to Holland Park, clump of bamboos at Map Ref 24777971—he should find half a dozen dead pigeons somewhere in there. Second, park gardener not turned up for work—if more than one, it's the guy who had roast peahen for supper last night. Yeah, peahen. I want an autopsy on all of them, pigeons, peahen, gardener. Hell, man, in that case I want the contents of his stomach. OK? Now the other thing is I think it

98

wouldn't be a bad idea if we could fix up some sort of doctorate for Mr. Humayan—we could do with a bit of status about the place, huh? Have a look through that research budget list, see who owes us a *quid pro quo*. Shouldn't be too difficult, they'll be glad to have him. You should have seen what he did to the big machine yesterday—tied it in knots."

"I am sorry about that," said Humayan, watching him put the phone down. "I was aware that there had been an overload, but not that it emanated from me. I am sure all my programmes were coherent."

"Yeah, sure. I don't understand these things, but you had our engineers hopping. Not your fault. Some sort of coincidence of coding which broke into another programme and set up an infinite loop."

"I see," said Humayan vaguely. Normally he would have traced the event to its source, out of sheer mathematical curiosity, but now his mind was fully occupied with running five magic syllables through and through. Doctor Humayan. Doctor Humayan. Mr. Mann was making another call.

"Hi, baby, who's in A3? OK, you've got half an hour to shift him out. Ring the Big Boss first, say I want it, because they're ... OK, OK. Then get all his dirty pin-ups off the walls, and have enough of Mr. Humayan's stuff fetched down from the Lab to make it look right for him to be working there. You may have to pad it out a bit—poster of the Taj Mahal or something, ring up the FO and get them to send round a signed photograph of Nehru. Anything you fancy, provided it looks real. Soon as you've got that going find some lass with a nice voice and have all calls to Mr. Humayan shunted through her —tell her she's his secretary. Give her List Five and get her to fix interview appointments, half an hour each, beginning 11 a.m. today. Only List Five—he won't have time for those other creeps. Great. Now, where were we?"

The last four words were spoken to Humayan, but Mr. Mann answered them himself.

"Yeah, I know. We'll leave your problems with Moirag for the moment. Thing is, we've had all Fleet Street

99

on the phone since breakfast, chasing you. I staved them off till I could brief you. We're going to dress it up a bit, give you a nobby office, all that. You don't mind?"

"It will be a great interruption to see them one at a time. Might we not hold a press conference?"

This had always been an ambition—to be a scientist of such calibre that when he announced a press conference the press actually came.

"Too dicey," said Mr. Mann. "You've got to face it, we're working in a pretty delicate field, and you haven't all that experience of some things in it. There's nothing harder to keep the lid on than a press conference. Somebody asks a catch question, you come out with the wrong answer, and they've all heard it—foreign press, too, and it's a bloody sight harder to lean on *them*. But you see them one at a time and there's less pressure on you so you won't give so many wrong answers. And if you do, we've only got that one reporter to lean on."

"How shall I know—how will you know if I've given a wrong answer?"

Mr. Mann grinned like a happy schoolboy, lifted a flap in the machine by his desk, selected and pressed a switch. A plaintive voice filled the room.

"...I say, I say, I'm trying to speak to the Director. Oh, thank God, Jake ... what? Oh, I'm ever so glad you liked it, that *is* kind of you ... But look, Jake, this is about a simply ghastly mistake which ... but there's a lot of *men* ... Oh, Jake, you don't mean that, this is serious, they've come into my room and started moving all my stuff up to a pokey little hole on ... You *knew* about it and you didn't tell *me*! ... Oh, Christ, careful with that! That's a Riley! ... Sorry, Jake, I was talking to the workmen. You know that rather nice Bridget Riley ... the black and white one ... Heavens, I don't know what colour *she* is. Do be serious, Jake ... Oh ... Oh, well, I suppose ... (*tinkle*) ... oh, Christ!"

Mr. Mann clicked the switch up. Humayan laughed, but woke no response.

"You can't choose the tools you have to work with," said Mr. Mann heavily. "I'm used to that. But some of the people you've got to work for! OK, Pete, that's all fixed."

He picked up another telephone, dialled, waited, asked for extension thirty-six, dialled, spoke.

"R5," he said. "Scramble? OK, Scramble."

He pressed a button on the instrument.

"Right? Good. Did you know you had an ex-C in your house? Yeah, that's her. Then why the hell ..."

He broke off and noticed that Humayan was still in the room. Frowning with his spare hand he made urgent motions of farewell, and a gesture to explain that Tarquin would cope with any problems. Humayan bowed and left.

A3 was a nice room with two big windows looking out over Somerset House. The carpet was soft and the books on the shelves quite convincing; the Telex was as good as his own, but had a seldom-used appearance; the poster was not of the Taj Mahal, but of an Oxfam child in a Calcutta slum; and the signed photograph was of Mrs. Gandhi. The journalists arrived at half-hourly intervals, allowing him a five-minute gap during which he could study the dossier on the next. The details were sparse and easily learnt, so he had spare time to play with the computer, coding all the personal information on each interviewer that he could glean from reading and observation. While he was doing this he discovered that the coding manual for this room was much more elaborate and detailed than his own, and covered quite a useful number of instructions for arranging and altering the work-priorities governed by the supervisor section of the big machine in the basement. This was trove! He put the manual on the desk and learnt off bits of it while his interviewers were making notes.

The man from the *Telegraph* had lived thirty years in India and spent much of his time asking after Maharajas and Test cricketers. The lady from *The Guardian* was prettyish but obsessed with polygamy and the subservience of Indian women. As soon as the man from *The Times* had settled his sharp-creased trousers to his satisfaction the door opened and a white-jacketed

Celt carried in a silver tray holding sandwiches, a jug of fresh orange and half a bottle of champagne. The man from the *Mail* got coffee—this was a sad figure who as almost his first assignment in Fleet Street had been detailed by a live-wire editor to dye himself green and see what the life was like; the dye had worn off but left him typecast as a specialist on Celtic affairs, which he was, a well of bored expertise. One of the men from the *Sun* spent twenty-three minutes taking a photograph, which left his literary colleague two minutes to scrape together enough facts for a caption. The man from the *Express* asked loaded questions about the hereditability of Celtic genes in the Royal Family. The rest, one way or another, asked Humayan what all the fuss was about, so he told them what they wanted to hear and they wrote it down, asking him how to spell the longer words. When the last one had gone he sat at the Telex and set it to print out his results. Mr. Mann came in while the machine was still chickering, and tossed a folded rectangle of paper on the desk.

"What are you up to?" he said.

Humayan studied the print-out. Even in this statistically negligible sample he found certain salient oddities.

"Those journalists," he said, "have had an average of 2.53 divorces and 6.9 jobs in the last ten years; 9.0909 per cent of them (that was the second man from the *Sun*) had any idea what I was talking about. A hundred per cent of them had dirty fingernails."

Mr. Mann's genial laugh pullulated through the room as Humayan stood up, locked the Telex and put the key in his pocket.

"We could have got you all that," he said. "It's in store already. And quite a bit more dirt than what's under their nails. There's not many of them we couldn't bring to heel pretty damned smart if we chose."

"I wouldn't have thought Mr. Leary..."

"Frank's different. Now, what do you think of this, huh?"

He flicked the paper with his forefinger. Humayan picked it up and found it was a telegram offering him a Doctorate in Anthropology at the University of East Anglia.

"That is very gratifying," he said stiffly. "Have you already replied in my name, too?"

"Well, I thought we might sit on it for a day. East Anglia's sound, and we've got half the dons there working on projects for us, but the faculty are getting a bit of a reputation for being blind whiteys. The way I look at it is this—you're the real thing. Anybody would be glad to have you, so we might as well keep East Anglia for a guy we've really got to unload. I've got Tarquin working on Cardiff—now, that would carry real weight if they gave something to you, huh?"

"I have in fact corresponded with Professor Evan Evans..."

"Now, he's a useful man. Knows which side his bread is buttered. Got that, Tarquin?" he shouted suddenly at the ceiling. "Old waffling Evans!"

"You needn't bellow," complained the child in the Oxfam poster. "This thing's supposed to pick up a whisper. My poor ear-drums!"

"OK," said Mr. Mann. "Now, Pete, your trouble with this servant-girl—I've fixed that."

"It will not involve any awkwardness between me and the Glisters?"

"Awkwardness!"

Mr. Mann stared at him. Humayan shrugged humbly.

"Hell, no," said Mr. Mann suddenly. "Everything's going to be fine. You can forget all that. What time are you going home?"

"Oh, very soon, I think. I cannot start any useful work now."

"Hey!" said the child in the poster. "There's a flash just in—they got those jokers who did Harrods last week."

"Great!" said Mr. Mann.

"Hang on, boss," said the child. "It wasn't them trying to knock the store out, it was an inter-green thing. It was the ICS cleaning out a CSI cell."

"Yeah," said Mr. Mann. "Knitting codes into the Fair Isle jerseys."

The child laughed.

"I'll be right up," said Mr. Mann. "Boy is that big machine beginning to pay off! So long, Pete."

A doctorate at Cardiff! From sheer euphoria Humayan celebrated by taking a taxi home, thinking as he did so about the day's dealings. In a curious way the most gratifying thing of all was the jug of orange that had come in with the champagne for the man from *The Times*; that they were prepared to consider *his* habits! This thought recurred to him several times on the journey, last time as the taxi slid down the long avenue whose pavement he usually trudged. He watched the familiar landmarks flash by and came to an unfamiliar one; a group of green workmen had the pavement up on the corner turning towards Horseman's Yard, and were at that moment arguing vehemently with the lanky street-sweeper. Perhaps it was this jarring note that echoed in his mind and raised sudden doubts: how had they known about the orange juice in the first place? Known that he was now calling himself Pete? Why did Moirag have an alias? Every mathematician knows the moment when a complex calculation diverges from what has hitherto seemed its natural course, the sense of wrongness which, long before the calculating layers of his mind have any real grounds for suspicion, makes him go back and check. This was such a moment. But the taxi swung into the kerb and he put his hand into his pocket for coins and brought out with them an intrusive key. The key to his own Telex was on his key-ring: this must be the one for the Telex in A3. Somehow his unease crystallised away from its real cause and on to this scrap of metal. He was still cross about his own absentmindedness when he walked in through the door of Number Six.

Doctor Glister was in ambush again in the hallway.

"Hi!" he said. "Come in and have a gossip. We've been reading all about you. I'm kicking myself for not having done a piece on you for *Prism*."

Humayan smiled with wary politeness and followed him into the living room. Mrs. Glister was there, smilingly reading Mr. Leary's article; she had untuned her tension one whole twist, and looked almost welcoming. Kate flopped across a chair, so succulent that Humayan was afraid he might have to visit Selina that evening, tired though he was and though he had not budgeted to afford her services more than once a week. Glenda was hunched against the wall like a suspicious foetus, as if she thought someone was trying to steal her new familiar from her.

"You're looking a bit beat-up, Pete," said Kate, as though that were the finest thing in the world.

"Catherine!" said Mrs. Glister.

"I have had a tiring day," said Humayan. "It is difficult to explain my sort of work to laymen, though they put me into a fine office to do so and gave the journalists champagne."

"Did they?" said Doctor Glister. "Then I must certainly do a piece on you."

"Apparently it depends on whether your journal is on List Five."

"I doubt if it's on list ninety-nine—we're not all that popular. What will you drink now?"

"Oran—" began Humayan, then remembered who would be squeezing the fruit. Glenda scrambled gawkily to her feet.

"I'll get it," she said. "I told you about Moirag, Dad. He's got to be careful. I hope you asked Mum to tell her to lay off."

"I can't do anything with her," said Mrs. Glister with a sigh. "But I promise you she's very loyal, Mr. Humayan. They never really mean it."

"How's Dick?" said Doctor Glister.

"Mr. Mann? Ah, he is very friendly and helpful. I have met nothing but kindness from the English."

"It's a nice place, I always say," said Mrs. Glister. Kate snorted and looked as though she were about to gather herself for some sort of flouncing onslaught on her homeland's niceness, which she so well exemplified, even to her compassion for all human suffering whose alleviation would not seriously affect her standard of living. Doctor Glister sucked a warning note on his pipe as Glenda slid into the room slopping orange juice down the sides of a tumbler.

"It's all right," she said. "I've drunk some myself, and I'm not dead."

"I'm getting tired of that particular joke, Glenny," said Doctor Glister. "You'll be putting ideas into Moirag's head."

"Dick Mann?" said Mrs. Glister. "Is that the nice boy you used to play cricket with? In that Home Office Team?"

"Same name, different lad," said Doctor Glister dismissively. Glenda must have sensed that he wished to change the conversation for she deliberately kept it going.

"You didn't know Dad was a mighty batsman, did you, Pete? We've got snaps of him knocking up centuries for teams all over the world. Would you like to see some?"

"Not now, Glenny," said Doctor Glister. "I want Pete to tell me how his work's getting on. Sit down, Pete."

Inwardly Humayan sighed—and then for the first time that day he found himself undergoing a close and intelligent inquisition about the progress and prospects of his work. Doctor Glister had evidently been doing some background reading—Humayan could recognise two of the books which had provided many of the questions—but he had also thought about the subject for himself. The difference between his approach and that of the other journalists (except possibly Mr. Leary) was that he seemed to think the subject mattered, apart from filling a few inches of next day's paper. In fact his approach was more like Mr. Mann's than anyone's, informed but wholly pragmatic. Perhaps it was no coincidence that in the course of his questioning he revealed a thorough knowledge of the inner structure and functioning of the RRB. Mrs. Glister too seemed to know the names of many of the people there, asking after ancient ailments or afflictions (including wives) from which they all seemed to have suffered in the old days when the world was young and did not realise its lack of innocence.

Occasionally Kate tried to intrude with belligerent remarks on the viciousness of the whole structure, but Doctor Glister brushed her aside with a wave of his pipe; Humayan considered this a very wholesome way to treat one's daughters, and began to wonder whether Doctor

Glister would be kind enough to dissuade Glenda from practising her witchcraft on his tenant. Glenda herself said nothing at all.

Nearly an hour later the door cracked open; Moirag was in no mood to use the handle. Humayan cringed from her green, Bedlam figure but she seemed hardly to notice him, swaying in the doorway, a warrior queen, chained and captive but dreaming of mad triumphs.

"Supper's on the table," she shouted, gave the room a lopsided curtsey and smashed the door shut.

"Oh dear," said Mrs. Glister, "she's not usually drunk as early as this."

"That's not drink," said Glenda. "She's up to something."

Humayan rose nervously, anxious to get to his room and lock himself safely in before Moirag had finished serving. The Glisters let him go. As he crept upstairs he wondered what on earth Mr. Mann had meant by saying it was all fixed.

For high summer it seemed a lowering evening, though it was long still until dusk. Humayan cooked savourlessly out of tins, then sat staring at the gymnasium wall, watching the colour seep from its yellow, mottled bricks. He tried to run through the previous day's calculations in his head, to acquire the momentum for a fresh bout of thought; but fear of the virago in the kitchen made the effort useless. After a while he heard the expected movement outside his door, and a soft knock.

"Who is it?" he called.

"Me, Glenda."

"Where's Moirag?"

"Washing up."

He opened the door a crack.

"It's the Miss World contest on TV, Pete. We thought you might like to come and watch it. Miss India's very pretty."

"No thank you. I am working," he lied.

He locked the door as she went away, but even so the intrusion was disturbing. He enjoyed beauty contests, but knew that the added stimulus would make it impossible to refrain from a visit to Selina later, and that would mean a return journey through the shadowed streets of midnight. He dared not risk that, but sat in the dusk and fingered the little collar for comfort. After a while he became aware of a new noise, other than the twitter of commentators seeping up the stairs; this came from inside the house; it was slow and careful movements from the next-door bedroom—Kate's. A bedspring muttered as it received weight. Now he could not hear anything and so was left to imagine the movements on the bed, the stealth that made each touch and caress tingle with an extra charge. He was tired. His morale was low. He wanted to see Selina but didn't dare. Really, he told himself, it would be asking for the superhuman to expect restraint of him in such circumstances. Very quietly he opened the cupboard door and removed the hangers that held his suits. A yellow needle of light speared through the spyhole. He was not surprised—with a girl of Kate's beauty you would want to be able to see the flush of excited blood welling into those soft cheeks. He eased himself on to the *Statistical Journals*.

It was Moirag who lay on the bed, fully dressed. She was drunk. The bedside light shone full on her green contorted face.

No, even in drink her head could not be at such an angle, nor could the blotch of scarlet on the pillow be any sort of alcoholic tipple. She was dead. Slain.

He fell from the cupboard, gulping. The whole Yard had heard his quarrel with her. She had tried to poison him. He had told ... These stupid, insular pigs of islanders would believe at once that brown men settle such matters with knives. He must ... He must ring up the Indian High Commission, yes. That was first. But not from this house. Not from this cursed house.

A smell of fireworks was in his nose as he staggered down the stairs, wrenching at the buckle of the little collar; he had it off by the time he flung the living room door open and could see the whole Glister family staring at the stupid parade. He threw the collar across the room at Glenda. It hit the wall above her head.

"You have failed to protect me! You have failed to

protect me!" he screamed. She was scrabbling to her feet with the collar in her hand as he rushed out of the room.

In the main road he stopped, shivering and panting, staring up and down under the plane trees and trying to remember in which direction he had seen a phone booth.

"Mister," said a deep voice.

He shook his head. The street-sweeper was moving hugely towards him, round the unfinished hole left by the workmen.

"Got a light, mister?" said the man.

"No, no, go away," said Humayan. But the man now blocked his way between the hole and the wall. Behind him he could hear a girl's footsteps running on the pavement. He started to move back, to go round the other side of the hole.

An enormous light, a wall of warm air, a long, colossal boom. The shock shoved him like a tidal wave across the pavement. He fell to his knees but raised his head to see whole fragments of building soaring through the still singing air, lit with orange from below, like leaves in the updraught from a bonfire. The green man had also fallen but was getting to his feet. A few feet further back a girl lay prone on the paving. He knew from her clothes it was Glenda. She held the little collar in her hand.

Over his gaping face a pungent darkness closed, stinging his eyes. A huge weight hit his back. Gasping he breathed in the chloroform and swooned into dark.

So he was wholly unaware of being stuffed into the street-cleaner's stinking cart. And the first neighbours to come running paid no attention to the familiar slave shoving his burden up the avenue, and barely more to Glenda's body lying stunned on the pavement. There were much more shocking and amusing things for them to see in the shambles that had been Horseman's Yard.

PART II

Greenside

VI

Dublin, Thursday. *At a Press Conference here today Mr. Gareth Jones, Information Minister for the Welsh Government in exile, blamed the deaths of forty-three schoolchildren directly on the Saxon forces of occupation. He said it was deliberate London policy to paint school buses the same colour as vehicles used for the transport of troops.*

This statement was immediately criticised by Mr. David Jones, Shadow Information Minister for the Welsh Opposition in exile. He said it was a typical piece of mealy-mouthed flannelling. The truth was that while the sacred sod of Wales groaned under the foreign foot the people of Wales had a holy duty to achieve maximum violence and disorder to symbolise their rejection of Saxon rule. The deaths of forty-three children was as good a symbol of this rejection as the deaths of an equivalent number of soldiers, and in some ways a better one. He was still speaking when a member of the audience fired three shots at him and immediately held an impromptu press conference to clarify the ideology of his action. Mr. Jones's condition was later said to be as good as could be expected.

The dreams of chloroform are menacing in their very ordinariness and solidity. A vault of whitewashed brick, a single bare electric bulb, two yellower sources of faint light at the limit of his upper vision; a dank smell; a bruised body with a special soreness round the mouth, as though he had shaved too closely and then daubed on an astringent lotion; fear.

After a long while he knew that all these, especially the fear, were too enduring to be dream stuff. Without moving anything except his eye muscles he explored the mysterious prison. The whitewashed vault at either end became a dark arch framing the ghost of his own nose. Beyond his feet the wall was divided into deep brick compartments about a yard square. Above his head the two brass knobs of the bedstead split the light into yellow rays. He stared at the right-hand knob. When he was twelve his mother had bought him a bed like this, ready for his wedding night; that radiant knob, and the fear, and the weakness of the drug (or drugs) combined to unlace the adult carapace and leave a soft child lying on the mattress, yearning with a child's fierce and hopeless rage for dark-skinned crowds and food with honourable spices reeking from it and the background odours of sun-cleansed dirt.

"Pravi," he whispered several times, but then changed the word to "Pete", using the Saxon syllable as a sort of mantra, repeated and repeated, to summon his soul back to here and now, to being a Saxon lying in a Gaelic prison on a brass bedstead with a pillow so soft that it seemed to have persisted out of dreams. The knob had been recently polished. Straining his eyes against the rays he was able to see, distorted by its roundness, the whole of the room reflected. He was alone. Only the two dark arches could hold menace. Very cautiously he moved his head to the right.

TWANG!

His muscles locked rigid, then melted slowly into tremblings when not a footstep answered the alarm; but the very relaxation must have altered the focus of his weight upon the bed-springs.

TWANG!

An inch of movement in any direction, with any limb, woke these tuneless harpings. The devils, he thought, the green devils. They have left me alone on this twanging bed so that they will know at once when I wake, and then they will come and beat me up and say I was trying to escape and put me against a wall and shoot me. But I will outwit them. I will outwait them. I will lie perfectly still until they come to see if I am dead, and then I will reason with them, in a dignified and fatalistic manner.

So he lay perfectly still for several hours. He did not feel like mathematics—his processes were not sufficiently coherent. Instead he became Pravandragasharatipili Humayan, a speck of being, who summoned into that speck the vast peacefulness of the universe. Occasionally on the fringe of his consciousness he was aware of the ghost of a man called Pete who would remark in a superficial touristy way that there were undeniable advantages in being an Indian, with hereditary resources and techniques available that were unknown to Western races. At first the appearances of the Pete-ghost were few and ethereal, a wisp of mist in the slow whirlpool of non-matter. But after many ages the mist began to draw itself into solidity, until at last it strutted into the sphere of peace and remarked loudly that Indians could be jolly interesting chaps if you were the kind of chap who was interested in that sort of thing, but they were hopelessly impractical about drains and that sort of thing, and for instance this chap with the impossible name was going to wet the mattress of his marriage-bed jolly soon if he didn't pull himself together and find somewhere to urinate.

Perhaps if he had practised more seriously at his hereditary techniques he might have been able to control and master both attacks, the dread in the mind and the piercing sweet ache in the genitals; but with a cry of despair Humayan flung back the blankets and leaped from the bed. The springs answered this convulsion with one colossal chord and twangled into silence. Nothing stirred under either arch.

Action, plus the altered position of his body, seemed to give his bladder fresh strength, which in turn gave his mind time to plan. The green devils could not know that he was not a sleep-walker, so ... He raised both arms horizontal before his face and stalked staring into the darkness under the left-hand arch. At once his nose told him he had come to the right place. When he stopped and looked about him he could see by the light behind that there was no enemy under this vault either—only a couple of buckets on the floor and another arch beyond leading into deeper darkness.

The bucket he chose was resonant enamel. The released water clattered on to the side like hail on a tin roof. It was a tocsin. Pleasure froze but still the stream slashed forth. The whole vault blazed with sudden light, and still Humayan stood there, trapped by the inexorable process, cringing for the blow.

Beside him loomed a purplish shape. He dared not look. A second tocsin rang on a slightly different note. In his peripheral vision he could see a parallel stream to his own clattering into the other bucket. Only when he was easing his zip up did Humayan allow his glance to flick sideways for a shy instant; still he did not dare look at the face, but the hands were enough, paler than veal and veined with blue. Furthermore the man had been circumcised. Humayan turned trembling from the buckets and waited for the man to finish, studying out of the corner of his eye the broad back and the ancient purple dressing-gown.

The man swung round.

"Hi," he said, "and welcome to gaol. My name's Zachariah Zass."

"P. P. Humayan," said Humayan, holding out his hand. Mr. Zass shook his head.

"We won't shake, I guess," he said. "I haven't washed for three days. Pickles are nice guys, but they have no notion of hygiene."

"Of course, of course," said Humayan, who was finicky about such matters himself.

"Had enough sleep?"

"I think so. What is the time?"

"No time down here, sir. Come in. I have a table and chairs my side, and we can talk."

He groped beyond the arch and found a switch, then turned off the light in the chamber with the buckets. This new vault was slightly larger than the others, and instead of having two dark arches in facing walls it had

116

them at right-angles to each other. The bed was similar to Humayan's, the table and chairs very plain and battered. Humayan, relaxing into physical and mental relief, noticed now how coldly the slabs of stone which floored the place were striking through his socks. He went and fetched his shoes from beside his bed, turning off his own light as he left. When he returned he found Mr. Zass already sitting at the table, wrapped in an extra blanket from the bed. Humayan sat opposite him and they studied each other without embarrassment, that being the natural thing to do.

Mr. Zass had not shaved for several days, but under the stubble his skin had a tended look, as did his hands and fingernails. He was pudgy but strong-shouldered. His tan did not look natural, and in any case was acquiring a greyish tinge, from beneath. His eyes were small, dark and bright, his hair sparse and close-cropped. There was a weight, a solidity about his personality that reminded Humayan of Mr. Mann. To judge by his voice he was an American.

"Yeah," he said suddenly, "we'll just have to get along with each other best we can. My friends call me Zack."

"Pete," said Humayan.

"Glad to know you, Pete."

"The gladness is mutual. Where are we?"

"I can't figure the geographical where, but I reckon this is the wine cellars of one of the lovely great houses they have in this island, which Mrs. Zass was looking forward to visiting. In the sticks somewhere, too. I've seen mud and bits of grass on their shoes."

"Who are they? What do they do? What happens?"

Humayan could not keep the note of fret and fear out of his voice, but Mr. Zass appeared not to notice.

"The pickles?" he said. "One of the guerilla movements, I guess, but don't ask me which. They treat us right, give us regular meals, though it's not what Mrs. Zass would like to see me eating. They'll be along soon. You don't have to worry, Pete, provided you play the game their way. No fancy footwork. No do or die. Just keep them happy and try to play it so it's in their interest to look after you. What did they collar you for?"

"I do not know. I am a medical statistician. I am working on the hereditability of the green gene, but my work is purely theoretical. It is true that a newspaper printed a rather sensational account of my work, but..."

"You don't know pickles like I do," interrupted Mr. Zass. "That's how they are. They see your name in the papers, something to do with genetics, and they're damned touchy about that, so they pick you up. Don't think what they're going to do with you, of course. Just the same with me."

"What happened to you, Zack?" said Humayan, asking for politeness the question in whose answer he had no interest at all. What was going to happen to *him*, that was what mattered. In his self-absorption it took him some seconds to notice that Mr. Zass had not answered him. He looked up, and saw on the heavy face a look of outrage, which slowly faded into pique, and from that into not-quite-genuine amusement.

"I happen to be the United States Ambassador to the Court of St. James," said Mr. Zass.

A maniac! The green devils had shut him in this horrible place with a maniac! Humayan jerked his chair six inches, realised that there was nowhere to flee to, gulped.

"I am honoured," he gabbled. "Very honoured indeed. I ... er..."

"Shucks," said Mr. Zass. "Perhaps it wasn't in your papers. They've got this censorship thing pretty tightly sown up over here. OK, I'll tell you. I wanted Paris, and Mrs. Zass wanted Rome, but the President said to me, 'Zack, I'm asking you to take London, because you know the pickles, and what's more they know you know them.' I didn't like it, but I took it because I knew what he meant. He meant he wasn't having his Southern strategy diverted by having to keep the East Coast pickles happy, more than he had to. 'Mr. President,' I said, 'how will the London Government take that?' 'Screw them,' he said—he's a fine man, Pete, when you get to know him —'Screw them. They've been on hot bricks that I was going to send them a pickle as ambassador. They'll lick your boots.' So what happens? I'm at my tailor in Savile

Row, having a fitting for my ambassador's uniform, cut-away jacket, knee-breeches, gold lace, cocked hat, when the fire alarm rings and we all run into the street, and there's half a dozen pickle gunmen and I'm sandbagged, and next thing I know we're here. So much for the vote of the East Coast pickles. So much for world opinion. Where are you from, Pete?"

"Bombay, India."

"Same thing. Indian opinion is world opinion too, so they hijack a distinguished Indian scientist. They don't stop to ask which side world opinion will take, or what good it will do them, because they're pickles. We'll have a Russian in here next."

Humayan began to relax. Mr. Zass's mania didn't sound dangerous—perhaps it had been induced by loneliness . . .

"Do we see much of our gaolers?" he asked.

"Sure," said Mr. Zass. "There's a guard in here most times, and when they leave us they pull the fuse, because there's not much you can try in the dark. I got 'em to leave the lights on last time, so you'd not go crazy when you woke up. You see, with pickles when they're reasonable they're just as reasonable as you or me. It's only when they aren't they aren't. That's . . ."

Beyond the further arch metal and wood jarred. A chain rattled. The darkness there blinked light.

"Yoohoo, Excellency," called a voice.

"Here," drawled Mr. Zass. "And Pete's here too. He's awake."

"Let's listen to the lilt of his tongue, then," said the voice.

"Yes, I'm here," croaked Humayan.

There was silence and stillness under the claustrophobic vaulting, and then a man sprang into view and posed crouching, well back from the arch, with a submachinegun jutting beside his hip. He wore a kilt and sporran and tartan stockings from the top of which a dirk projected beside his green knee. The ectoplasmic features of his stocking mask were topped by a jaunty green bonnet. Leap and pose, the mask that did not mask the passionate aggression of the stance—they were those of a devil in a dance, a devil from a Tamil

119

ballet, a green devil. The gun's black muzzle swung from prisoner to prisoner.

"Ay, mon," he said. "Baith there, a' douce and sonsy."

"Come off it," said the first voice. "Megan, darling!"

A far snarl, female, answered. Another man sauntered into sight and through the arch. He held a large pistol loosely in his right hand and leaned against the brick-work. He wore a mackintosh, cloth cap and knitted green mask, that covered his whole head.

"Good morning, Excellency," he said. "Good morning, mister."

"Glad to know the time of day," said Mr. Zass.

"Yes, it is morning," said the man, "and all dewy with the tears of the cherubim and the air as soft as bog-paper. Or perhaps it is night, with the skies all orange from the glow of neon where earth's sinful cities anticipate hell. Will you turn that gun aside now, Ian, man? I do not wish to see our Megan injured in the backside. We Welsh have a fastidious notion of honour."

He was answered by a sniff, but not from the man in the kilt. A dumpy little woman came into sight carrying a tray which was laden with crockery and shrouded objects. She stumped forward under the arch for a few paces, then halted. Though her features were indecipherable under an elaborately crocheted mesh her whole pose spoke outrage. She swung aside, still clutching the tray, and darted across to the Welshman.

"You were not telling me it would be a black man," she said in a whisper loud enough for the echo of it to come whispering back from under the furthest arches.

"Ah, come on, Megan, honey," said Mr. Zass. "Pete's a good guy and a famous scientist too."

"Oho!" said the Welshman. "And from which twig of the many-branching tree of knowledge does the little bugger dangle?"

"I am a medical statistician," said Humayan.

"There, Megan," said the Welshman. "The house is honoured. A man whose profession is the enumeration of bunions is a man we are proud to have under our roof."

"But will he be cleanly in his habits?" whispered the woman.

"Hygienic beyond dreaming," said the Welshman. "He brushes his teeth between mouthfuls, and his religious code is such that..."

"Hold it," said Mr. Zass. "Let's leave religion out of this."

"Oh, I am not superstitious," said Humayan, nervously eager to placate. "If you could read my horoscope you would see it says I am not superstitious."

The Welshman chuckled.

"This voter is a humorist," he said. "You will be needing your dyspepsia tablets, Ian."

The Scot grunted. Megan carried the tray to the table and laid out with great precision a number of little paper doilies on to which she placed the plates and saucers. There were more doilies to protect the cups from contact with the saucers, and the plates from the food, which was wrapped in individual portions inside paper napkins. Finally in the exact centre of the table she placed a white jug from which steam arose, then put her palms together in front of her veiled mouth and spoke.

"Lord who decreed
Leaf, fruit and seed,
Watch that we feed
Only our need.
Save us from greed."

"Amen," intoned Mr. Zass, slavering slightly. As Megan turned away with another sniff he rapidly undid the little packages in front of him. Humayan followed suit. Knife, fork, spoon and teaspoon were separately wrapped; there was even a mysterious parcel that seemed to contain nothing, until he realised that it was a paper napkin wrapped in another paper napkin. Where the parcels contained food it usually had an inner wrapping provided by the manufacturer—sugar cubes in individual packaging, tiny rectangles of butter in foil, sliced meat loaf in plastic, a polythene bag of rolls. Mr. Brown put his tea-bag into his cup and poured hot water over it from the jug.

"Meg's not yet invented a way of wrapping water,"

said the Welshman. "But you're working on it, aren't you, sweetheart?"

"I will not have them thinking that because we are a poor people we are not cleanly," said Megan, polishing with such fury at the already gleaming knobs on Mr. Zass's bed that all the springs stirred and tinkled. The food was almost savourless and the water too tepid to drag anything but a little colour out of the tea-bags. Mr. Zass ate rapidly and carelessly, and when Megan had finished with the beds and came stumping back to clear away she paused and sniffed.

"An ambassador ought not to be making so many crumbs," she said. "What would the Queen be thinking, if you were sitting by her, strewing your food about in such a manner? 'Mr. Ambassador,' she would say, 'you will be bringing the mice into my palace.' And she would mean it, though she might smile, for she is too well-bred to speak to you of the sinful waste of it, and the boorish behaviour."

There was no hint of teasing in her voice. Either the green devils had deluded her also, or Mr. Zass really was an ambassador.

"Pete's a tidy eater," he now said, defensively.

"One millionth of a starving million," explained the Welshman. "That's how he was brought up—not to go tossing his crumbs about in case he needed them tomorrow."

Curiously, Humayan sensed that when Megan came to collect his share of the crockery she was not appeased by his neatness, was indeed disappointed to find no debris at his end of the table, though she rubbed with vigour at invisible spillages. The Welshman escorted her and her tray out under the arch. As soon as the metal of the far door rattled and snapped the Scot lowered his gun point, scrabbled with his free hand in his sporran and withdrew a twisted cigarette which he stuck through a ladder in the stocking and lit one-handed. His relaxation was only marginal; there was still something poised and wary about his hold on the dangling gun. The Welshman returned, carried a chair from the table and stood on it to reach down from the highest compartment one bottle, two mugs and a packet of drinking straws. Mr. Zass fetched from a lower compartment a water pitcher and two tumblers.

"Scotch, mister?" said the Welshman.

"I do not drink alcohol," quavered Humayan, terrified of offending the demons. But their response, visible only in their stances and audible in a joint grunt, seemed to be a mixture of contempt and relief. The Welshman poured out three measures of whisky, pierced his mask with a straw and took a contented suck. The Scot muttered a fierce toast in an accent too broad for comprehension, drank, and banged his mug down on the table.

"What's into you, Ian?" said the Welshman.

"Wull-brred, is she?" muttered Ian.

"Who?"

"Megan was saying she was wull-brred."

"Megan Pritchard? Man, she has a very fair breeding, clear back to Seithenyn ap Seithin Seidi, and many of them branch bank managers."

"Her Majesty the Queen," snarled Ian. "Megan was saying that she was wull-brred."

"A figure of speech," said the Welshman. "A touch of hyperbole."

Ian threw his cigarette to the floor and ground it out with his foot.

"Gentlemen," said Mr. Zass, "I am an ignorant foreigner but I had always taken it as an axiom that the Queen has the best pedigree in England."

"In England, verra like," admitted Ian.

"But there's two of her own great-great-grannies she cannot put a maiden name to," said the Welshman.

"Och, there's waur than that," said Ian. "The leddy is full o' gude Scots blude, but ne'er a green bairn she has born, nor any of her predecessors."

"Not forgetting the Welsh blood also," said the Welshman.

"Och, aye, but there is mair o' the Scots."

"Tudor," said the Welshman coldly. He had laid his pistol on the table while he drank, but now his fingers crept across the deal towards it. "It is the quality that counts," he hissed.

"Aye, aye," said Ian, too lost in his argument to fret for details. "Stuart is maybe no verra gude. But there's been green bairns born in plenty behind palace walls, Mr. Zass, only the English bishops have smuggled them awa and brocht in some bonny Saxon bairn. Generation after generation it has happened, so in what manner can her present Majesty be callit wull-brred? For a' anybody kens her true name is Ruth Potts, and the richtful king o' Scotland is lockit in a tower."

"It's not often you meet a Maoist-Monarchist," said the Welshman admiringly. "I'm a republican, sober; but I'll give you this, Ian—you'd only need one generation to purify the blood."

"And in any case," said Mr. Zass, "I understood it was possible for the parents to have a considerable measure of Celtic..."

"Pickle, to you," snarled Ian.

"OK, OK, sure, pickle blood without necessarily producing..."

"Pickleninnies," said the Welshman.

"Sure," said Mr. Zass. "Isn't that right?"

"But the odds, mon, the odds," snapped Ian, pouring out three more tots and then marking the level in the bottle with a pencil he drew from his sporran.

"I read in the paper," said the Welshman, "where there's a little brown citizen been working on the odds. A breakthrough, it said he'd made..."

The silence of startled considerations took him. His mask swung round to stare at Humayan.

"Was that you, mister?"

"Indeed it was," said Humayan, gratified that his fame should have seeped as far as this remote cranny.

"And what for should a lousy oriental be researching my genes?" shouted the Welshman. "Are there no scientists in Cardiff?"

"Yes, yes," babbled Humayan. "I have corresponded with Professor Evan Evans, and he has expressed himself..."

The Welshman's snarl cut him short.

"Pardon me," said Mr. Zass heavily. "I intend no criticism of your organisation, but it seems irregular

124

that you should snatch a guy like Pete and not know who he is."

Both gaolers made a sudden slight movement. Humayan realised that their masks made a warning glance unreadable.

"Can the gentleman tell us, forbye," said Ian, "what odds it is Her Majesty should bear a green bairn?"

"I could do that," lied Humayan. "I would need certain data. As much as can be discovered about the racial origins of her forebears, and their physical appearance. Her ear and jaw measurements and those of her husband —these would need to be very accurate. Otherwise only the standard vital statistics."

"Aye," said Ian in a tone of doubt.

"And then what?" hissed the Welshman. "We send in the burglars to the royal dentists. We waylay the Duke and measure his buttocks. This joker gets out his sliderule and says that Her Majesty's next will be as brave a green as ever bracken was, so we set about increasing the royal libido. You'll have plans for that, no doubt."

"Haud your thrapple," said Ian. "It is the historical fraud that maun be brocht tae licht, and if the brown gentleman can dae it ..."

"Goodbye to your FRS, Pete," said Mr. Zass.

The Welshman appeared to lose patience with the argument. He picked up the mugs and bottle and hid them back on the top compartment, nodded to Mr. Zass and left without another word. Mr. Zass settled down to playing cribbage with Ian. Humayan, exhausted with fresh fears, went and lay on his bed and brooded unconstructively on the bitterness of being kidnapped by green demons who didn't even know who he was.

VII

Cork, Thursday. *For the second day running the World Conference of Celts broke up in disorder, with no business conducted, having again been unable to reach any compromise on the controversial Cornish resolution concerning the shape of the earth. By a procedural device the minor nations, Cornwall, Brittany and Andorra, have managed to block all moves to by-pass this resolution and proceed to more urgent matters. For some time this morning it appeared that the Conference might accept a Scottish motion stating that the so-called roundness of the earth is a falsehood foisted upon the Celts by the Saxon Newton and the Jew Einstein, but postponing for further consideration any declaration of what shape the earth in fact is. This move was blocked by the Cornishmen, who genuinely appear to believe that the earth is flat, and the Bretons, acting on orders from Paris, according to well-informed quarters. A move to appease the hard-liners by expelling the New Zealand delegation, who have all along maintained that the earth is round and that they live on the far side of it, had no result except a walk-out by the New Zealanders, thus removing from the Conference its most level-headed element. After break-up it was being rumoured that this was the result for which the Irish had been working, in order to exclude the New Zealanders from later debates in which their moderate counsels might have prevailed. Some indeed now think it likely that the Cornish motion will be passed with no further difficulty tomorrow morning.*

Time ached away. Meals came. They ate, slept, excreted, talked, lay in dark silence.

There was a rough roster of three gaolers, Ian, an excitable little Welshman called Ossian Jones, and a white student. The first Welshman, whose name was Dave, appeared to be head gaoler, coming for a while at the changes of duty, drinking a couple of tots when it was Ian's turn, and then going away. Mr. Zass tried steadily to make friends with all of these and had some success with them, apart from the student. He would play cards and argue with Ian and Ossian, deliberately losing by the end of each session. Indeed at one point he allowed Ossian to win so large a sum of notional dollars that the Welshman fell off his chair in a sort of fit, and the prisoners were in the predicament of having an unconscious gaoler and a perfectly usable gun.

"I guess not," said Mr. Zass, gazing regretfully down at the weapon. "We'd not get ourselves free before Dave comes back, even if we rub Ossy out ... Oh, forget it. Hell!"

With a sigh of relief Humayan knelt by the twitching body and bathed the temples in cold water. When Ossian came round he made no reference at all to his fit, and Mr. Zass sensibly told him that they'd added an erroneous nought to the original bet, which made it an acceptably smaller sum.

The student refused to talk or play cards, because he was reading for a Ph.D. He also insisted on the prisoners sitting as far as possible away from him and talking in whispers. They learnt from Ian that he was at ideological odds with the rest of the group, being a supporter of the Universal Celtic Language, which combined elements of Gaelic, Welsh and Irish and was favoured by the more rigorous revolutionaries despite the disadvantage of being at least two-thirds incomprehensible to almost all Greens. This dispute in the movement was the only one they were told of directly, but in Ossian's remarks, especially, there were frequent implications of schisms and fissions all through the hierarchy. Mr. Zass was too canny to press for details.

As soon as Dave was out of the room the student used to tug his mask off his head in order to be able to read his textbooks without strain. This revealed a pale, elongated face and a straggle of ginger beard which looked as though it did not really belong there but was part of the fleece of some large russet sheep which had snagged on the student's chin as the animal passed. His voice had an upper-class bleat, which Humayan had last heard from the lips of a very old British Council lecturer in Bombay.

Mr. Zass, the first time this visage appeared, nodded towards it and whispered, "I didn't care for it, till I found what small fry he was."

"Oh," whispered Humayan, "why not?"

"I reckoned they wore masks because they intended to let me go. If they'd been planning to rub me out, they wouldn't have bothered. They can't wear them all the time."

"Why should they, er, rub you out?"

"You can never tell with pickles. Course, I know if they do rub me out it'll be a quick shot in the back of the head. But I keep seeing it as a firing squad. They line up in the middle of the court, see, and I'm against this wall, and I say 'no, no blindfold,' and the officer asks if I have a last request and I just mumble, so he comes closer to hear what I'm saying, and then I kick him in the crotch. I used to be a pretty fair kick when I was at college. What do you think of that, Pete?"

Humayan smiled politely at this display of hypothetical guts. He found Mr. Zass tiring company. It was not exactly that the big Jew was arrogant or boastful, but very few conversations proceeded without casual references to his wealth and power. The reason, for instance, why he had a reputation for understanding the Greens was that his chauffeur, his manservant and all his gardeners were green. He had travelled far but narrowly, visiting only cities that contained a first-class American hotel and there seeing only those sights that were rated five stars in the guidebook. Any restaurant he had eaten in was the best, any man he mentioned was a great guy and any woman a very lovely lady. Humayan was bored with these achievements when he believed them to be the delusions of a maniac, and when he found that they were probably true he became both bored and jealous.

This revelation came on what might have been Humayan's fifth day in the prison, when Megan brought in to breakfast some black clothes glittering with threads of gold and laid them on Mr. Zass's bed with a dismissive sniff.

"Thanks, honey," said Mr. Zass. "That's great. You see, Pete, when they sandbagged me I had just run out of this tailor's shop in my court dress, only they hadn't finished the fittings so it was all white thread and chalk marks, so Megan's been finishing it off for me. You couldn't have done a better job, honey. As good as Savile Row. My tailor used to make your Duke of Windsor's jackets, Pete, but the Duke had his pants made over in New York. There isn't a tailor in Europe knows how to make a pair of pants."

Humayan, wondering in what manner the Duke of Windsor could have been said to be his, watched Mr. Zass struggle into his finery and strut like a flabby rook around the cellar. The absurd cocked hat looked equally irrelevant whether born on the head or tucked under the arm-pit. It was indeed galling to think that this was the Ambassador of the United States of America, whose acquaintanceship might have been most useful to a rising statistician, given other circumstances.

So after that Humayan spent a lot of time on his bed. In any case there were the long hours when the green demons pulled the main switch and left their prisoners unguarded in the dark. Humayan had never needed much sleep, so now there was nothing to do but lie awake and dream, or think, or meditate. Sometimes he worried dully at the enigma of how he had come to be kidnapped by revolutionaries who did not know who he was; sometimes he thought about Selina, or Kate, or Mr. Palati's curries, but mostly he considered the programming of the big machine in the basement of the

RRB. If any help came, he decided, it would start from there. That was the only creature in all Britain (apart from Mr. Palati) with whom he had been able to build a comfortable relationship; he could talk with it in a way he never would be able to with Mr. Zass. So he lay in the dark, remembering that friendship, reconstructing it by systematically listing in his mind all the coding instructions and references he had seen, and then trying to work out their relationships. The task was impossible, even for a genius. Humayan's memory for figures was complete and effortless, but it was linear. He could not carry a mass of figures at the front of his mind for mutual comparison, but had to summon small batches from his memory store, juggle with those and see what he found. Even so he made progress. After several of the dark, trance-like sessions he became aware that given more data and a calculating machine—pencil and paper would do —he could have unravelled the whole maze.

About the time when he realised that he would make no further progress and so was sitting whispering small-talk to Mr. Zass—their relationship remained uncom-fortable because there was no area in which he could give this intensely competitive man the satisfaction of com-petition—Ossian Jones came to relieve the student in a very frenetic condition, brandishing his gun and a news-paper in wild arcs.

"They've done it! They've done it!" he shrilled.

"Hold it," said Mr. Zass. "You got that safety-catch on?"

Ossy must have heard, despite his frenzy, for he checked by pulling the trigger. The bullet whined and flicked round the vaults while the slam of the explosion dazed their ears. The noise calmed him enough to make him drop the newspaper and prod dazedly at the safety-catch. The student picked up his books and left.

"Wales won some kind of football match?" said Mr. Zass, unfolding the paper. His face changed and hardened as he read. Ossy was beginning to moan, "They've done it! They've done it!" again before Mr. Zass finally passed the paper across to Humayan.

It was the paper Frank Leary worked for, and the

relevant story was written by somebody called Jack Courage, who was described as the Celtic Affairs Correspondent.

U.S. APPOINTS GREEN ENVOY TO LONDON
"QUEEN WILL RECEIVE HIM": Foreign Sec.

The text added little. For politeness Humayan read hurriedly through paragraphs about this new nonentity, who appeared to have spent his life making himself rich and then being the statutory green man on a number of state and federal boards and commissions.

"What does it mean?" he said.

"It means I'm an ex-ambassador now," said Mr. Zass. "Our friends here aren't going to like that, any more than Mrs. Zass is. I wonder what you'll make of this Mahoney guy, Ossy. He's a real bastard, and the Mafia owns fifty per cent of him, too."

"They can appoint a sheep, provided he's green," said Ossian exultantly.

"They will let you go now," said Humayan.

"You reckon so?"

"They have no use for you if you are no longer ambassador."

"Yeah. But they've been outmanoeuvred. They won't like that. They've lost face."

"But they have gained face by having a green ambassador presented to the Queen."

"Except it's Mahoney. You know, Mrs. Zass used to worry herself sick what I was going to say to Her Majesty. At least Mahoney can talk race-tracks with her. Hey, Ossy, what's that?"

They had all three heard it, a signal from the door, only ten minutes since the last guard-change.

"Stay here," hissed Ossy, sliding his safety-catch over and moving cautiously away. He went with theatrical stealth, like a child playing grandmother's footsteps. They heard the clatter of the door-fastenings and a short bout of talk, made somehow menacing by the rising note of Ossy's excitement. Then the fastenings clattered again and there was silence. After a couple of minutes Mr.

Zass walked round to the entrance and returned, shaking his head.

"Gone," he said. "I don't like it."

"At least they've left us the lights," said Humayan.

They sat for a while, listening to silence. The change of routine was very disturbing. Humayan kept imagining that he could hear the far noise of gunfire. Mr. Zass picked up the paper and read as though his eyes had starved for newsprint, missing nothing, and occasionally making muttered comments such as "Kaiser Al are down," or "Edible brassières, huh?" It might have been an hour later when he folded the paper carefully, passed it across the table to Humayan and tapped with his forefinger a little item low down on an inside page.

The Race Relations Board have informed the Indian High Commission that an Indian subject, said to have been working in the RRB statistical department, can definitely be regarded as among the victims of last month's explosion in Horseman's Yard, Kensington.

A successor has been appointed to Doctor Gideon Glister, editor of *Prism*, who was another of the victims. The new editor will be Mr. Tarquin ffoster, a Civil Servant with a strong interest in Celtic Affairs.

No progress has been made in discovering the perpetrators of the explosion. A woman is still helping the police with their enquiries.

They hadn't even given his name! He who a fortnight before had been fanfared on the trumpets of Fleet Street as a world-famous scientist was now a defunct and anonymous member of the statistical department! He was shaking with rage as he passed the paper back.

"You didn't say about the explosion, Pete," said Mr. Zass.

"I had forgotten it, but now I remember the noise, and a roof floating up through the sky ... they are all dead. All my friends are dead."

"That's too bad, Pete."

"Even the dogs are dead."

"Now, that's a very English thing to say. Course, I've heard that some of you Indians are more English than . . ."

"The dogs were horrible," snapped Humayan. He stalked out of the cell, past the acid-smelling buckets, and lay on his bed in the dark.

At first he did no more than surrender himself to the miseries and dreads that gusted round the cavern of his being. His right hand crept for comfort to his left wrist, to fiddle with the amulet that he no longer wore. The face of the witch who had given it to him swam before his eyes, calling. Glenda had been running along the pavement clutching the collar. So she was not dead, then.

But Doctor Glister was, and Mr. Leary—for his paper now had a new Celtic Affairs Correspondent—and Moirag. But Moirag had died before the others, with her throat slit on Kate's bed. Too many deaths, too many deaths.

Humayan felt suddenly irritable with the untidiness of it all. In such a short space of time one housemaid had been murdered, a household had been blown up, and an Indian visitor senselessly kidnapped. It was easy to imagine many motives for murdering Moirag, but not there, in that fashion—and whoever had done it must have come and gone along the ledge, which was Mr. Leary's private road. Humayan was considering Moirag's look of mad triumph as she announced supper that last evening, when the light in his section of the cellars flicked on.

"Let's try and get us out of here, Pete," said Mr. Zass.

"Impossible," said Humayan.

"It's a kick to nothing, Pete. Listen—that's shooting. My guess is that's your police come to look for us, and we're hostages. Maybe we can't get clear, even if we do find a way out, but perhaps we can hide long enough for them not to use us the way hostages do get used when the chips are down. And if they weren't intending to rub us out—hey, I'll still be able to tell Mrs. Zass I tried to escape. You never met a woman wants to respect a man the way Mrs. Zass does. Come along, Pete—I had a look

133

round that first night they brought you, when they left the lights on."

As if in symbol of leadership Mr. Zass settled his cocked hat firmly on his head and strode off under the further arch. Humayan padded sulkily behind. In the next compartment there were no wine-bins; it ended at an open door, beyond which was a room with a blackened floor across which three stone partitions projected from the right-hand wall, making four short, narrow alleys. At the end of each alley a square door was set high in the wall, fastened with a big bolt that was held in place with a padlock.

"Coal-chutes, I reckon," said Mr. Zass. "See how that lintel slopes? They opened the doors and shot different kinds of coal down the chutes, so they must lead outside. And see what I found."

He poked with his foot in a shallow heap of coal-slack and uncovered an S-shaped hook, pointed at each end.

"If I put a bit of an edge on this I reckon we can gouge that bolt free. You go fetch a chair, Pete, and then stand sentry by the main door."

Humayan watched him remove his hat and braided coat, squat down and settle like a cave-man to a steady scraping of his hopeless tool on the flagstones. Then he went obediently off to fetch the chair—he could always claim, if they were caught, that he had had nothing to do with the escape attempt.

Sitting cross-legged like a Bombay beggar with his back against the stonework by the big door, he tried to order his thoughts again. From far he now distinctly heard shouts, and the occasional shot, which disturbed the analytic process. Furthermore a mind used to sawing through the clean-grained stuff of numbers goes jerkily into the knots and flaws of human timber. But he persevered, driven mainly by the growing knowledge that he, P. P. Humayan, had been treated as a naïve idiot by practically every Saxon with whom he had had any dealings. A banked-up stream of anger kept the millwheels of his mind turning.

He thought about Mr. Leary. It was a nuisance his

being dead. If he were alive, it would be clear that he had
murdered Moirag and then blown up the Glisters' house
to conceal the body. Moirag had been spying on him;
Humayan had betrayed this by shrieking about knowing
her wickedness; Leary had questioned her and she had
tried to blackmail him—hence her look of mad triumph
when she had announced supper. He knew the way along
the ledge. The 'books' which the fake postman had de-
livered were explosives. Leary knew about explosives and
explosions—he had waited for one to happen that other
evening, by the children's playground. Moirag had been
blackmailing him about the brand on his shoulder—that
made the meaning of the symbols clear.

And Moirag had an alias on her card. And Mr. Mann
had sent for it from the computer without referring to any
directory, as though it were a variant on a code he knew
well. And then he had talked on a scrambler phone with
a senior colleague, whose extension was the same as
Doctor Glister's, thirty-six, talked about the colleague
having an ex-C in his house. And Doctor Glister had
played cricket all over the world, and he wrote the small
ads in *Prism* himself, and the copy in the waiting room
of R14 was next month's, and the big computer had
known about Humayan's orange juice. And Doctor
Glister, that strong and intelligent personality who
worked at what seemed to be a half-phoney job, had gone
far, far out of his way to attract a lodger who would be
unwelcome to his wife, and then force her to accept the
fact.

But even Mrs. Glister had been less despised than he,
Humayan, had been. She had been allowed to know about
the explosion in the knitwear department at Harrods.
Many of her friends had been RRB officials—and Mr.
Mann had known her, even known her dogs enough to
dislike them. Or had it been the Glisters he disliked?
He had known Dr. Glister had the Enoc ap Hywel disc,
with the RRB stamp beneath the label—and that the
Glisters called Humayan 'Pete'; and it had been Doctor
Glister who suggested that Humayan should get the pass
that carried that name. So the editor of *Prism* seemed
almost to live in the pocket of the head of R14. And the

135

new editor, Mr. Tarquin ffoster, had come out of that pocket.

Humayan turned these thoughts round and round in his head, arranging them in patterns. The most coherent pattern still had several large pieces missing. He thought again about Mr. Leary and the scar on his back, and his relationship with the RRB, from whom he had even got the photograph to illustrate his article on Humayan. "Frank's different," Mr. Mann had said. And that was true. Frank had made one half-hearted attempt to conceal his closeness to the RRB, but he had not cared much, because . . .

"You gonna try a shift, Pete?" said Mr. Zass; he was standing, streaked with sweat and coal-dust in the doorway to the coal-cellar, and his lips looked an unlucky colour. Humayan took the S-shaped hook from him and went unwillingly to his task.

It was a cruel tool. With the sharpened point one could gouge out, by careful effort, a single small splinter of wood. Ten such splinters would have made a matchstick. The door was oak, nearly two inches thick, and the old bolt was held to it with nails that ran its full depth. There was nothing for it but to gouge clean round the bolt.

Time, deranged before by the behaviour of their warders, now became meaningless, to be counted in rests, in drinks from the water pitcher (or in Mr. Zass's case in swigs from Ian's whisky-store) and in the imperceptibly swelling pile of sticks that grew between the chair and the wall. As Mr. Zass grew drunker so his drive became more furious. He screamed at Humayan for the little he had done in his shifts, and lurched on to the chair and tore at the tough wood. Humayan screamed back, and wept, and did sentry.

At last he heard a shout from the coal-cellar. Prickling with terror that the bolt had come loose, the door was open, and Mr. Zass had promptly betrayed them by his triumph, Humayan rushed round, to find that the ambassador had fallen off the chair and was lying groaning on the floor. The whisky bottle was empty. Humayan helped the drunken swine to his feet and led him to his bed, on to which he fell without even a grunt of thanks. Bitter with rage Humayan returned to the bolt.

Ten minutes—two hours—three days later, give or take a lifetime, the bolt came loose, wholly unexpectedly, where a hidden split in the timber ran exactly along the line that still remained to gouge. With shaking fingers Humayan eased wood and bolt and lock away from the door, out of the stone and free. The whole door then opened with a groan, and beyond it a tunnel of stone sloped up and ended where the sweet night stars began. Very quickly he shut the door again, scared that some sentry might have seen the upshot beam of yellow electric light. Shivering with the thought of desperate deeds to come he went to shake his leader awake and tell him that the road to freedom lay open.

His leader was unwakeable, gripped in the coma of alcohol and exhaustion. Humayan even wasted a few drops from the water-pitcher to sprinkle the broad brow, but Mr. Zass only muttered, "Not just now, honey," and rolled away while the bedsprings played their tinker's serenade. Several times Humayan stole back and forth between the bed and the chute, nerving himself to make the break alone and finally not daring. At last he chiselled some mortar from a crack, mixed it into a paste with spittle and coal-dust, wedged the bolt back in its place and filled the gouge-marks with his paste. He swept the pile of chippings into a corner and covered them and the hook with coal dust, cursing the fate that had bound him at such a moment to this drunken American hog. There had been no mention of any such detail in his horoscope.

He could not sleep. He could not even rest, though he was almost delirious with fear, hunger and exhaustion. Numbers chased themselves meaninglessly across his mind. He prowled the cellars, grinding his teeth. Faint light showed round the cracks of the chute doors. He cursed again. How he would speak to Mr. Zass when the swine awoke! As a symbol of his contempt he snatched up the ambassadorial hat and put it on, though its rim came over his ears. He was still wearing it when he heard, on the other side of the main door, the first sounds of rescue.

Voices muttered. A hacksaw whined into metal. The gaolers would have used a key! He croaked a welcome. The sawing stopped. Voices spoke. The lilt of Welsh was unmistakable.

Humayan tried to beat his fists against his temples but was impeded by the ambassador's hat. He took it off. The sawing continued. He did not know what to do, but so strong was the urge for action that he put the hat on again.

At that moment the sawing ceased and the door rattled open. Humayan, posed under the electric bulb with his whole face shadowed by the hat, confronted a group of men, masked and armed, posed under the dawn-lit arch.

"You this ambassador feller, mister?" said one of them in a voice so pinguid with geniality that Humayan knew at once that they were here to set Mr. Zass free.

"Sure, that's me," he said in his best American.

"And a grand morning to you," said the man. The four of them moved towards him. He wished he could have seen the smiles under their masks—poor peasants, they were not accustomed to the company of the élite of the diplomatic corps.

"OK, boys," said the man suddenly. Two of them leaped forward. A soft, dark bulk knocked the hat from his head and at the same instant smothered his head and shoulders. His hands were seized and roped behind him. But after the first quake of terror he neither struggled nor protested, realising that it was only natural that they should want to conduct him from their hideout in such a manner that he could not tell the police anything useful. Moreover, he was now anxious not to wake Mr. Zass.

Unnamable birds twittered in the sweet morning air. Humayan could hear them even through the sack over his head, and smell the sap of things. It was cold. He waited, swaying with tiredness and nerves. He could not steady the swaying.

"Stand up, won't you?" said a man, catching him

138

round the shoulders to stop him falling for the second time.

"I cannot balance! I cannot see!" he shrilled.

"Ach, take the cloth off him then," said another voice.

Five seconds later Humayan stood blinking and smiling at the dazing day.

He was standing on the side of a hill, on a large rectangle of fine-mown turf. Behind him and on two sides were stone walls which retained the earth where the hill had been cut away to achieve this terraced level. Plants, mauve and yellow and white, trailed in brilliance down the stone. A dozen men and two women, all masked, were conducting a low-voiced discussion a few feet away to his right. Most of them had their backs to him. Further away down the hill, in the only direction he could see out, lay an ornamental lake over which a faint dawn haze hung in bands. Two rowing boats were working on the lake in conjunction with a small group of men on the shore; the work seemed to involve taking a series of long, heavy parcels out into the middle of the water and dropping them over the side of the boats. When his eyes stopped blinking Humayan saw that the parcels were bodies, and that the reason that they looked like parcels was that the party on the shore were lashing them thoroughly to concrete fencing-posts so that they would sink and stay sunk. The lake was as pretty as anything Humayan had ever seen, with different coloured rhododendrons flowering and reflected along the further shore, the grey dome of a tiny temple emerging from the torrid flowers and the dark green of the leaves, and further up the lake two perfect swans surging towards the boats to see whether the activity of the humans involved any edible fragments.

"Right," said the man who had so far given all the orders. "Stand him over by that wall there."

The group took up some sort of formation, with a line of men to Humayan's left, the women and leader and one other man opposite, and the rest in another line on his right. A tall white man took Humayan by the arm and led him to the back of the rectangle; looking down at the hand that gripped his elbow Humayan saw that the top joint of the index finger was bent almost at ninety degrees to the rest of it. There couldn't be two hands like that, so battered, so red. But it would be a mistake to jeopardise his own chance of freedom by any sign of recognition—and Mr. Leary must have been of the same mind.

One of the women took a small notebook from the pocket of her jeans and read from it in a clear gabble. The regional accent had been ironed off her voice and replaced by that of the emphatic intellectual. Humayan only half listened. The phrases floated in and out of the daze of his hunger and exhaustion. The last of the bodies down on the lake was being swayed overboard. It wore a kilt.

"...ally of racist neo-fascism ... crypto-genocide ... cultural violence ... April the Fourteenth ... so-called conciliation ... United Nations resolution ... arms shipments ... conspiracy of capitalism ... dollar investments..."

She ended, it seemed, in mid-paragraph, as though her speech was something that was extruded from a word machine and could be chopped off anywhere.

"Well, does the feller plead guilty or not guilty?" said the leader in a desultory voice.

"Guilty," said the other woman.

"OK. Sentence?" said the leader.

The group to Humayan's left all raised their hands.

"Death," said the foremost of them.

"Fine," said the leader. "Firing party."

The group to Humayan's right mooched round into a line opposite him. He heard the faint click of safety-catches.

"No, no!" he screamed. "You are making a mistake! I am not the ambassador! The ambassador is asleep in the cellars where you found me! Mr. Leary can tell you I am not the ambassador!"

His hands were still tied so he pointed with his toe at the tall white man with the battered hands.

"Hold it," said the leader. The guns came down.

"I was thinking the newspaper photos were no' verra like," said someone.

140

"You know the feller, Number Eight?" said the leader.

"Sure," said Mr. Leary. "He's an official at the RRB."

"Then why the fucking hell didn't you say so?" asked the leader. "We've wasted half an hour trying the bugger. Firing party."

"No! No!" screamed Humayan. "I am not guilty! I am a pure researcher! I am objective!"

The guns levelled.

"I can tell you who caused the explosion at Horseman's Yard!" he screamed. "No!"

He flung himself to the grass. The world was black and filled with clamour. Then it was still.

"Pick the feller up," said the leader. "Hang on to that other feller."

Humayan was hoisted to his feet. Memory began to tell him that only one gun had gone off, and now in the shocked and reeling morning he saw that two of the firing party were holding Mr. Leary's arms, and one had a pistol to the stockinged temple. The leader strolled towards Humayan over the beautiful turf.

"Now, will you tell us what the hell you are talking about?" he said fretfully.

"Yes, yes," gabbled Humayan. "I was residing in Horseman's Yard, at the house of Doctor Glister, next door to Mr. Leary there. A maid of Doctor Glister's tried to blackmail Mr. Leary, because she discovered that he was an RRB agent. He has the letters branded on his shoulder. He killed this maid and then blew up the house to conceal the fact, trusting that it would be thought that it was the work of guerillas, because Doctor Glister was really the secret head of a section of the RRB called R5. I can explain all my reasoning..."

"The hell with reasoning," snarled the leader. He crouched as if he were about to strike Humayan, then swung round.

"Let's see his face then," he snapped.

One of the men dragged the cloth mask off. The craggy face stared forth, contemptuous.

"Sure, I bombed Glister," said Mr. Leary. "He was boss of R5."

"And why did you try to shoot this brown feller?" said the leader.

"Balls," said Mr. Leary.

The leader kicked him on the knee-cap, hard, without causing any flicker of pain to cross his face.

"We'll have that shirt off," said the leader.

The muscled torso looked strangely raw in the raw, pale light. Heads craned at the symbols.

"H.R." said somebody. "That's the old Hieland Railway."

"No, no," called Humayan anxiously. "Look at it the other way up. That little cross doubles the R."

"Could be," said the leader. "Any of you fellers seen anything like this?"

"There was a group in Liverpool, you see, used to brand people. I remember my own Dad arguing it was more moral than shooting."

"OK," said the leader. "We'll shoot the both of them, then."

"I appeal to the Council," said Mr. Leary. "I have their orders for everything I have done."

"He'd be saying that anyway," said one of the women.

The leader's hand rubbed his stockinged chin.

"I'm not risking it," he said after a pause. "But I'll see you die untidy, mister, if you've been lying to me. We'll just shoot the brown feller, then."

"No, no!" screamed Humayan. "The Council will need me as a witness."

Somebody laughed.

"The witness system is a crypto-bourgeois obstacle in the machinery of the people's justice," explained one of the women.

"Firing party," said the leader.

"No, no! There is much more I can tell you. I can tell you about Mr. Mann. I can give useful information about the functioning of the RRB. I can..."

"Hell!" said the leader. "It's not my morning for shooting people. You five, there, take 'em away. Fetch this ambassador out and we'll shoot him. We can't waste any more time."

"We have already tried him," fluted the intellectual

woman. "He has pleaded guilty *in absentia*."

"That's something," grunted the leader. "Lock the big one up in a place of his own, and two of you guard him. Put the brown boy back where you found him."

VIII

And when all is prepared let the new initiates be brought in, naked, to stand before the Chief of the Sept. And let him say, "For what come ye, my brothers?" And let them say, "For vengeance we come." Then shall the Chief mark the brow of each initiate with the dung of a man and say, "On whom seek ye vengeance? For what crime?" And let each answer, "We seek vengeance on the Saxon who has made us as dung." Then let the Chief dip a cloth in the blood of sacrifice and touch with it the dung upon each brow, saying, "How shall this dirt be cleansed?" And let each answer, "With the blood of the Saxon. With the blood of the Celt. If I slay not, may I be slain." Then shall the Sergeant lead them ...

Humayan sat on his bed, shuddering with shock and horror. In his ears still rang Mr. Zass's last inebriated bellow: "I'll do it, Pete! I'll do it!"

Though the shudders would not lessen he began in a despairing way to wonder what he could tell these murderous apes that they could actually understand would be useful to them. What could he buy his life with, having sold Mr. Zass's? But Mr. Zass would have been shot in the end, anyway. You do not have to be a statistician to calculate that if you have a chance to save one life out of two you should take it, even if that life is your own.

At last the doors rattled and he heard the shuffling of several feet. A group of masked men carried Mr. Zass's body into the other cellar and laid it on the bed. Mr. Zass groaned.

"What happened? What happened?" whispered Humayan, cringing by the archway.

"Broke his ankle," said somebody with a laugh. "Kicked Pat in the crotch and broke his ankle. You can't shoot a feller with a broken ankle, not if you're going to leave his body in Grosvenor Square to greet his new nibs. People might think we'd been beating him up. We've got our image to think of."

"I wouldn't like to do Pat's peeing for a week," said someone else. They were all laughing as they left, a jovial team.

"Pete," groaned Mr. Zass. "Come here, Pete."

Humayan crept across, wondering how he could defend his betrayal.

"Pete, I know what you tried to do for me, and I want you to know I think you're the greatest guy who ever lived. Greater love hath no man than this, Pete . . ."

Mr. Zass fainted.

Humayan was attempting to change him out of his court clothes into his old pyjamas when more men came, including a silent, competent Scot who set the ankle without anaesthetics and secured it with splints. Humayan asked timidly for food, and quite soon it arrived, less hygienically wrapped than Megan's but no more appetising. When he had eaten he went to his bed and slept the enormous sleep of shock and exhaustion.

The new gaolers did not leave a permanent guard, nor did they turn off the lights at night; on the other hand the impression they gave was of being rougher, less amateur, less affable. They brought meals more regularly than the previous gaolers, which made it possible to estimate the passage of time, and to treat the longer interval between tea and breakfast as night. On the third morning they brought a mattress and threw it down in the corner of the vault where Mr. Zass lay, and then carried in the unconscious body of Mr. Leary and laid it on the mattress.

"You can take care of him, mister," they said to

Humayan. "It won't be long. We're shooting him as soon as he can stand."

"We're not the sort to shoot a sitting canary," said the smallest of them; when they left he was still expounding to the others the pungent wit of the phrase that had been vouchsafed his lips.

"Who the hell's the new guy," said Mr. Zass. In his voice was the slight resentment of any sick patient when a yet sicker one is brought into the ward.

"His name is Francis Leary. I think he was some sort of spy or informer for both sides. I think they have tortured him."

Humayan had no experience of merely physical brutality, one man deliberately hurting another as much as possible. The big brutalities of disease and starvation he knew like old cousins, but this was different. There was a blotched and bruised look about Mr. Leary's face, and dried blood by his purple mouth; his left hand was a tangle of blood, and when Humayan knelt to make him more comfortable he found that the body below the rough blanket was naked, and pocked all round the nipples with small circular burns. Humayan sponged the face and dribbled a little water between the puffy lips.

Three men brought lunch. One of them lounged over to the inert figure on the floor and kicked it in the ribs. It responded no more than if it had been dead. The kick was poised again when Humayan screamed.

"Animal! Animal!"

"What's into you?" said the man, turning and forgetting to kick.

"You are making yourself an animal," said Humayan in a shaking voice. "Kicking a man who cannot even feel your kick. You are diminishing your soul."

"The swine's a fucking traitor," said the man. "It's him's the animal."

"I will not stand for it!" said Humayan. "I will not."

There was terror in his voice at the things his tongue had been saying to this armed brute, and he cringed as the brute lounged back to him, reached out, tweaked his ear, laughed and strolled away with the others. The bolts of the main door rattled dully home.

146

"Thanks, Pete," whispered a voice from the floor.

"You tried to shoot me, to kill me," said Humayan furiously.

"You can see why now. Forget it."

Humayan's fury ebbed into mere crossness as he ate the tepid canned stew, the flavourless stale bread, and the soapy cheese. It was too bad that he should be forced to entertain humanitarian feelings for this man who had tried to assassinate him in order to pervert even the rough justice of the guerillas. Mr. Zass's ankle was hurting him, so he spoke little. Humayan chewed and brooded on the unfairness of his fate. The stew was too unpleasant to finish, so he took the plate across and knelt by the mattress.

"Can you eat?" he asked coldly.

"They left me a tooth or two, yeah. Little, soft bits."

It was a slow process, insinuating the chilling shreds between those lips, and he was still at it when the guards came back for the plates.

"Jesus!" said the man who had done the kicking. "That's a bloody waste of protein. If he's well enough to eat he's well enough to be shot."

"I must have some disinfectant cream," said Humayan.

"For that trash!" scoffed the man. "Jesus, the bacteria won't have time to get going."

"Animal," said Humayan without turning round or raising his voice.

The man laughed and tweaked his ear again. Leary refused more food, so Humayan retired to his bed and lay in the dark, trying to wring more secrets out of the RRB computer. Liking to know, that was one thing. Needing to know, to save your skin, that was another.

The men who brought the last meal of the day also brought a tube of antiseptic cream. They called Humayan the Lady with the Lamp and tweaked his ear abominably, as if trying to prove that this moment of mercy was an aberration. Mr. Zass was of the same mind.

"Pete," he said, "I know you tried to save my life, so you may be some kind of saint, but you're wasting your time trying to help that scum on the floor. He deserves

147

what he got. And what he's going to get."

"I do not like him," said Humayan. "He tried to kill me. He is no business of mine, but I cannot think while he is lying there like that. Perhaps this is because I am a healer. It says in my horoscope that I am a healer, and I have not healed anybody yet."

"Mrs. Zass reads the astrology columns pretty assiduous, but I've never been able to swallow any of that stuff."

"My horoscope is just as true as most of the idiocies you Westerners believe," snapped Humayan as he settled to his abominable meal. Fastidiously he sorted out the edible bits and ate them slowly, as if the action were some ritual of purification. Then he made Mr. Zass comfortable and finally settled down to anoint the tortured body on the floor. It was a sickening task, and became more sickening the more of it was revealed. The genitals were hardly recognisable as any such organs. But the cream must have had mildly analgesic properties, for Mr. Leary kept muttering, "That's better. Ah, that's better." And when the job was over he lay on his back staring up at the vault with sane, wide-awake eyes.

"I'm better than those other sods," he said. "All those other sods."

"Why did you do it?" said Humayan shrilly. "Why did you do it?"

"Me? I made a trap and walked into it. I'm a journalist —I wanted to *know*. I got recruited. An agent knows more than an innocent, and a double agent knows more than a straight agent. You're safe while you keep your balance, because then you're too useful to both sides for them to smash you. I've fallen off before—this is the third time I've been through the grinder, but no one's broken me yet. You don't fall off unless you choose—you remember we walked round that Zone, Pete? Those fellers standing about, just standing about, empty as beer cans —that lad with the broken nose—'tis nae coward blude —they pushed me off. They made me take sides again."

"Moirag pushed you off," said Humayan coldly.

"She was a stupid greedy bag."

"And the Glisters? Kate? What had she done to you except loved you?"

"You think she was innocent? She only had to open her mind a crack to find out what her Dad was up to, but she wouldn't. That's not innocent. How did you find out he was R5?"

"Various ways," said Humayan. He had no wish to converse more than he need with this wounded but still dangerous beast—but somehow he still desired that the beast should admire him and could not forebear to add a sliver of evidence of his own new perceptiveness.

"A man called Tarquin ffoster is the new editor of *Prism*," he said.

"Yeah," sighed Mr. Leary. "Dick Mann was always trying to suck R5 in to his bit of the organisation. You get an outfit like that and they spend as much time trying to carve each other up as they do on their real job."

"Your people don't seem much different," said Mr. Zass. "What are this new lot? What happened to Dave and the rest?"

"There was a shoot-out," sighed Leary. "That other lot were Celtic Independent Socialists, and we're Independent Socialist Celts. You'd need a year's schooling to understand the ideological difference, but the real difference is that they were soft and we're hard. When I finished at Horseman's Yard I decided I'd gang up with the hardest lot I could find, and they're it."

This was depressing knowledge. The three of them absorbed it in silence.

"If there was a way out of this hole you wouldn't be here," said Mr. Leary suddenly.

Humayan looked at him without answering, but his face must have betrayed him. A light glowed in the mean eyes.

"Tunnelling?" sneered Mr. Leary.

Indifference was impossible. Humayan feared and detested this man, but even so was compelled by the sheer energy of life in the tormented flesh. Mr. Leary was vermin, trapped and maimed but still snarling. If he had complained, or even asked to be forgiven, Humayan would have found it possible to be merciless; as it was the emotional dilemma gusted him about. If he freed the vermin from the trap he would infuriate the trappers.

149

He sucked his lips in and out, trying to think.

"Who are this Council you appealed to?" he said at last. "Where are they? How can I talk to them?"

"You? They don't know you exist. They're in the house, sorting themselves out after seeing that CIS lot off, but they won't have time for *you*."

Humayan thought again.

"Suppose you were to get free," he said at last. "What would your plans be? Would you contact Mr. Mann?"

"Christ, no. He'd pull me to bits. I'm no use to him now, and I know things that aren't good for him. I'll shack up in the Zone, lie low for a few months, get abroad."

There was a sudden weariness in Mr. Leary's voice. It was as if a traveller, plodding bravely along an apparently endless track, had suddenly seen far off a possible end to his journey, and only then discovered that he might be too exhausted to reach it.

"All right," said Humayan. "I will help you escape, but I will not come with you. You must rest now."

"I'll need some clothes. The ambassador won't be wanting that clobber for a bit, will he?"

Mr. Zass woke from what must have been feigned sleep.

"Pete," he said, "if you let that no-good scum take my uniform, I'll never forgive you. Nor will Mrs. Zass either."

"Please, Zack," said Humayan. "I wish him to go. I have a plan for our release, without danger. But first he must go. Please will you trust me?"

"OK, OK," said Mr. Zass. "I'm not entitled to wear it any more, I guess."

Mr. Leary slept like an athlete after a race, as though there were no more problems in the world. Humayan woke him at what he guessed to be midnight, and anointed him again with the soothing cream. Then he helped to dress this murderer in knee-breeches, ruffled shirt, cutaway coat and stockings. Even the buckled shoes fitted fairly well. It must have been painful, but the only sign Mr. Leary gave was that his once ruddy face became so pale that in the end he looked like the ghost

150

of some dissolute earl, returned to haunt the cellars of his mansion. Mr. Zass, mourning his finery, said no word. Mr. Leary leaned hard on Humayan's shoulder as he staggered along to the coal-cellars.

While he was resting Humayan went and scrabbled in the pile of coal-dust. Suppose their gaolers searched it was important that they should not find the gouging tool, or it might seem that Mr. Leary had not made his escape without help.

"You will need a weapon," he whispered.

Mr. Leary grunted softly and took the hook. He felt the sharpened point and grunted again. Humayan switched off the light and lifted the bolt free. He swung the door open and there were the stars again.

The guards came early and angry. Humayan was hauled from his bed and stood in his shirt against the wall, shivering with fear that they would notice how bruised and scraped he was from the struggle to heave Mr. Leary up the coal-chute. He was fearful too lest by daylight they would find traces of his mortar in the gouge-marks, though he had done his best to clean it all out, and so would deduce that the bolt had been cut free some time before. But they were too busy cursing to look for clues. One of them kept saying, "Cut Dai's throat out, and I wouldna ha thought he could crawl." Dai appeared to have been the man who had stood sentry over the guerillas' cars.

A gross man, hunched with menace, came and stood two feet in front of Humayan. He just stood there, silent and faceless.

"Ye helpit him!" he shouted.

"No, no!" quavered Humayan. "He had a sharp hook and he held it to my throat, but I would not help him. He wanted me to go with him, but I would not. I must see the Council."

"Must ye just?"

"Yes, indeed. I can tell them Mr. Leary's plans. I can tell them whether they need move."

"I dinna want to move," said another man in a worried voice, like a clerk fretting about some little adjustment in office routine. The big man swung towards him, then swung back to Humayan with a movement that showed how his fist lusted for the smash of flesh. Faceless though he was, anybody, even Humayan, would have known him for a slow thinker.

"Och, ye'd better be seeing the Council," he said, as though this were his own wholly new notion.

Outside the cellar wooden stairs led up to a swing door covered with green baize which was held in place by a pattern of brass studs. Beyond this was a hall floored with polished wood from which another staircase, vast and swirling, rose to a remote plastered ceiling. Nowhere was there a carpet or one stick of furniture. Masked men moved about with the rush of crisis, carrying ammunition boxes and files of papers. The fat man led Humayan down a wide passage to a door guarded by a masked sentry. The two ectoplasmic faces whispered together in the shadows, then the sentry knocked a deliberate pattern of raps on the door and let them through.

This was a moderate-sized room with a large table in the middle. A woman and four men sat at the table; two of the men were white; none of them wore masks. This sudden appearance of the real faces of his oppressors instead of the ghost-faces of nylon and the devil faces of cloth gave Humayan a momentary pulse of courage. A radio was playing softly in one corner of the room, and a small green man was hunched over it. Apart from him the Council looked relaxed and businesslike.

"This laddie," said the fat man, "spoke with the traitor before he left. Say what happened, mister."

Humayan told them all he thought it was necessary for them to know. He could not read their faces, but was suddenly struck by the notion that they could not read his: each was alien to the other. The woman asked all the questions.

"He'd say that anyway, Leary," said one of the white men.

"Aye, but it has a likely sound," said one of the Greens. "Anything at all there, Alan?"

The man by the wireless waved a negative hand.

"If he'd got through to them, they'd be moving by now," said the woman.

"He might hide out first and then give them the tip anonymous," said a green man.

"He would not do that," said Humayan.

They all looked at him.

"He told me he is finished with Mr. Mann. He told me the Greens are his people."

One of the green men laughed.

"Thanks, Jock," said someone. "You can take him away now."

The big hand gripped Humayan's shoulder and flicked him round.

"No!" said Humayan, twisting his neck. "I have something much more important . . ."

"Ye do what the Council tells ye," said the fat man, whisking him towards the door.

"The big computer at the RRB," shouted Humayan as the door swung open.

"Jock!" said the woman's voice. The grip loosened. He was allowed to slink back.

"Well?" said the woman. "We are busy. Be quick."

Humayan stood upright and swelled his chest a little.

"My name is P. P. Humayan," he said. "I am the best medical statistician in the world. Easily the best. I was brought to England by the RRB, because of an accidental discovery I had made about the hereditability of the green gene. They hoped to use my work to extrapolate the population growths of the two races on this island. Do you understand?"

Their murmurs were of assent, but not of interest.

"Now," he said, more loudly, "to be a statistician of my calibre you have to be able to work very closely with computers. This I find easy. I understand computers very well indeed. In my office I had a Telex which allowed me to use the big RRB computer on a time-sharing basis. One day when I was talking to Mr. Mann—you know of him?"

These murmurs were quite different.

"Good, well that morning he told me I had been tying the big computer in knots. This of course was nonsense, just a manner of speaking; something I had been doing, my personal code of information storage, caused a very minor blockage, a little local overloading, in the circuits. You understand?"

"Sure," said one of the men, "but if you can tangle it up by filing away a few figures, why doesn't it spend all its time in knots?"

"Oh, the blockage I caused lasted only a few thousandths of a second. The machine then rejected the material, as it was programmed to do. It was also programmed to report the matter, which is how Mr. Mann knew of it. A machine of that type is full of all sorts of safety devices to prevent it getting tied in knots. It has what is called a supervisor circuit to control these safety devices, and also to allot the timing of all the various tasks which come in from different inputs. This supervisor circuit is very complex, it is the heart of the whole machine. I propose to show you how to put a rat into it. An electronic rat."

"What good will that do?" said the woman. "They will buy themselves a new machine."

"First," said Humayan, "that itself would take time. A year or more. Second, I do not propose to make the machine break down. I propose to make it a little unreliable, so that they cease to trust it. At the moment the whole organisation is completely geared to the reliability of the computer. I mention a name of a Celt to Mr. Mann. He taps some keys. Three minutes later he has in his hand the dossier and photograph of that person. Now, just to cause a doubt in his mind whether the dossier is the right one, to force him to check by slow, non-electronic means, that in itself will be a considerable achievement."

The oratorical vibrations of the last phrase seemed to hang in the dusty curlicues of the ceiling. The man who had laughed before did so again.

"I like it," he said. "You may not know this, mister, but one of the educational areas absolutely closed to citizens of Celtic origin is computer technology. Even if they get on to us, the fact that we've been trying it out will shake them."

154

"Sounds like wishful thinking to me," said one of the white men. "How the hell are we going to get a Green in, so he's even allowed to touch a computer. One hell of a screening, they get."

"That is certainly the first problem," said Humayan. "But I think I can help you. The woman in charge of the cleaners at the RRB is called Marge, and her sister is a professional prostitute called Selina who works at a house in Snide Street called the Daffodil. Selina told me that her sister is terrified that the RRB might discover what is Selina's trade, because apparently she would lose her job. So perhaps I can give you a bit of a lever here..."

"But a *cleaner*, mister," broke in one of the Greens.

"It is all right," said Humayan. "You must find me two things: first, the keys that were in my pocket when I was kidnapped. One of these is the key to the Telex in A3, which I believe has access to the supervisor circuit, and is a room not used by anybody who does any serious work. Then you must find me a woman who has no subversive record and is good at mathematics—not brilliant, but just reasonably good. *I* can remember every number I have ever seen, but I am not asking for that.

"Now, I will tell you what the computer technicians at the RRB will do when things start to go wrong. First there will be a conflict between the engineers and the programmers, about whether there is a machine fault or a programme fault. They will try to settle that by running the programme through an identical machine, but there is only one identical machine in the country, Mr. Mann told me, and that is at the Treasury and very busy. It will take them at least a fortnight to discover that it is not a machine fault. Then they will start looking for a programme fault, a coincidence of numbers which sets in train unintended computations. At this stage we will feed in a series of instructions that appear to point to a man named Tarquin, who used to employ the computer for calculating the odds on complicated bets on horse races. He is Mr. Mann's ADC, and extra-curricular work such as he has been doing is just the sort of thing that leads to coincidental failures of programmes. I must point out that it is not necessary for these instructions to be fed in at particular times. It is possible to instruct the machine to act in a certain manner whenever a certain series of numbers crops up, say in a pass, and also to reinstruct itself to do the same next time, while destroying the source of the original instruction. For instance, Mr. Mann's own RRB pass number ends with the figures eight-three-seven. The machine could be told that whenever it was asked about a number whose last-but-two figure was eight and last figure was seven it should supply instead information about Mr. Mann himself. This would therefore happen on average one time in a hundred. It is a typical, if very simple, coincidence error. The instruction that caused it could, I believe, be made to appear on analysis to have come from a Telex where someone had been fooling around with betting on horses. This is what they will start looking for, and therefore when they find it they will believe that they have now traced the problem to its source. However, other, similar errors will begin to emerge. They will trace them, by similar means. They will build a clock into the machine, and start to try to account for every instruction given it. Even this I believe it will be possible to circumvent. But in the end they will begin to think that perhaps the errors are being deliberately caused. They will trace them to the Telex in A3."

"And get our girl?"

"Not at once. It happens that the normal occupant of A3 is a rather foolish young man who has a homosexual relationship with the Director of the RRB. Mr. Mann hates him and would be glad of an excuse to break him. I think your cleaner will be able to recognise when that happens and escape, if necessary in such a fashion that it is clear that she was responsible for all the trouble. Not counting the further errors she will be able to leave behind in the instructions of the computer, I would be surprised if the whole process takes less than six months. And it will leave behind it a great aura of distrust. Very few people in the RRB who use the computer truly understand it. Their relationship with it is emotional and mystical. They will never quite trust it again."

156

"It still sounds like a fairy-tale to me," said the sceptical white.

"There must be some feller we could ask," said a Green. "Even if he's not up to this feller's level, he can tell us whether it sounds right."

"Blind him with science, this guy would," said the first man. Humayan agreed, but silently. There were unlikely to be a dozen people in England, and all of them Saxon, who could follow the details of what he was proposing to try to do. The room hung silent except for the faint, dotty gushing of the disc-jockey through whose outpouring the message of warning might come. It made a very sinister background.

"The proposal is ideologically sound," said the woman suddenly. "It is a logical extension of the tactics of urban guerilla war, to use the system to disrupt the system. This lackey of the system will teach us how, because he knows that if he is lying he will be punished."

"And we'd only be risking one agent," said the sceptic.

The man with the tendency to laugh did so.

"We haven't heard the lackey's side of the deal," he said.

"It is irrelevant," said the woman. She reminded Humayan in an odd way of Kate Glister, a Kate who had never been pretty, never been loved, never been killed. The man laughed again; what had first seemed a sign of humanity was clearly only a mannerism, like a sniff.

"Yeah, no deals," said the sceptic. "We can get it out of him."

"You are mistaken," said Humayan, only a little shrilly. "I am not brave, but what I have to do is very difficult—it will demand all my powers. If I am afraid I cannot think. If I am hurt, perhaps I will never be able to think about it again. I have told you that I can remember every number I have ever seen, and this will be necessary. But if you associate fear and pain with the task perhaps I shall suffer retrograde amnesia."

"Glib little sod," said the white man who had not so far spoken.

"Let's hear his deal," said the sceptic.

"Our listening to it does not commit us to considering it," said the woman.

"Oh, I have a very neat little package for you," said Humayan, relaxing almost into a salesman's wheedle. "You do not trust me and I do not trust you, yes? So I will not ask for my freedom at once, and I do not propose to start instructing your agent at once—in any case I have at least a week's thinking to do—I must not conceal from you that the task still presents many difficult and unsolved problems. So first you will demonstrate your good faith by releasing Mr. Zass, and then I will demonstrate mine by teaching your agent how to build an electronic rat. Finally you will let me go, because my real work is important to you, in ways you will never understand. OK?"

"Bollocks," said the sceptic. "Zass can tell 'em enough about this place for them to work out where we are. And then we won't have him as a hostage—we'll just have this wee brown feller. We'll have the Conciliators out here in twenty-four hours."

"Mr. Zass is a very honourable man," said Humayan. "He believes, too, that I tried to save his life at the expense of my own. He will not say anything that is likely to harm me. If you were to release him out of reach of Mr. Mann—perhaps in Ireland?"

"Here we go again," said the laughing man, sighing through his laugh. "We voted three each way, to shoot him or to let him go, and then we tossed for it."

"The Council cannot go back on a decision," said the woman. "It would impugn the reliability of future decisions."

"Huw won't like it," said the sceptic. "He'd set his heart on that firing-squad, the moment he saw that bit of lawn. He should have been running a theatre."

"Balls to both of you," said one of the white men. "I hate Celts. You always want to decide everything in terms of ideology or drama."

"It's in our bloody blood," said Alan, looking up from his crouch by the wireless. "Someone else come and listen —it's that sod of a Saxon who keeps putting on rhythm 'n' pibroch."

A shuffle took place, Alan exchanging stations with one of the white men, who crouched patiently over the radio waiting for some signal of doom to penetrate the mushy thud of the discs. Alan was a wiry, intent, cranny-featured Green. He had that cocky look that is often found in members of a suffering race who are not at the moment suffering themselves. He was a survivor.

"I vote we give it a swing," he said at once. "Look, we can ship the ambassador back on the boat that's bringing the guns. Pegeen can give him a nice deep sedative, and he'll wake up in the US Embassy in Dublin, in the ambassador's bed if we can lay it on..."

The next fortnight turned out to be the happiest Humayan had ever spent in his life. With Mr. Zass's manly farewell still aching through his fingertips he was settled down in a neat little room on the top floor of the enormous, empty mansion; he was given a dozen pencils and reams of yellowing paper, a bed, a table and a chair. For four days he lost himself in an abstract world, wrestling over the unknown miles with the many-tentacled monster in the RRB basement, till he could almost feel the chill of the air-conditioning that surrounded it and hear the everlasting dull whine of the fans that kept the dust away from its circuits. He had more information to work from than he had expected, for the erratic resources of the guerilla movement had pilfered a considerable number of RRB documents, from Arts Council subsidies for Eisteddfodau to confirmations of execution orders in Conciliation camps, from the sales of Scotch whisky in Japan to the illegitimacy figures in Llandaff. Each document bore its computer coding at the top and, like the army of ants in the fairy-tale who rescued the princess by each bringing one grain of rice to build the required pyramid, was another tiny grain of fact, and also of insight into the habits of mind of the men who had programmed the monster.

Food came, but sometimes another meal would arrive before Humayan had even looked at the first. One night he did not leave his chair at all, but thought the hours away till light came again, enough for him to see the smear of dawn mist above the lake where the bodies of Dave and Ian and the student lay decomposing. None of that fretted him at all. On the fifth morning he yawned and shivered and sent word that he was ready for his pupil.

Her name was Anna Lewis. She had been chosen because she had at one time sat through an economics course at the University of Wales, and had been heading for a First before a change in the Celtic Education regulations prevented her from taking a degree in that subject at all. She was a square-shouldered, sturdy little woman, whose black hair was streaked at the temples with grey. Her green face seemed to be all in one plane, with only the sharp small nose projecting from it. Her mouth was small and her teeth tiny and white, but her grey eyes behind heavy spectacles were large and round. She was very intelligent.

Humayan had not of course been able to plot out a complete and infallible course of action. What lay before Anna was a series of branching paths; at every point of fission she had to ask a riddle of the monster, and interpret its riddling answer, and then cajole or trick it into destroying all record of her passage while she groped on along the path the riddles had indicated. The task would have been impossible if Humayan had not already deduced the probable choice at all the nearer branchings and many of the further ones.

But that first morning he had to give up to preliminaries; he had drawn a careful model of a Telex keyboard, and little pictures of all the switches, screens and gadgets she would find around it. She asked the right questions, so in an hour he was able to start explaining the basic principles behind what she was going to have to do. She took on trust what she could not grasp and made sure that she understood what she could. He was able to leave out huge areas of knowledge that even a second-rate computer programmer would consider essential, because she had just this one task before her and would never need to know those things. By mid-afternoon he could take her to the entrance of the invisible labyrinth.

Hours later, when the light from the setting sun lay heavy and bronze across the lake, he felt her concentration suddenly slacken. They had been sitting all that time side by side at the table and now, as he too shook himself clear of the dream of numbers, he saw that her arm was hairier than his; the fine hairs gave a shot-gold lustre to the green. She moved her hand slightly so that the back of her green hand lay against his brown wrist.

"Ah, heavens," she said, "I could be doing with a good screw. You will think me a very forward woman, Pete."

In the Welsh manner she made both statements sound like questions. Humayan yawned, looked at the lake and then at the papers on the table, and considered. If his gaolers had a hidden camera somewhere in the room they would be able to take a photograph of him copulating with a Celt, and then would have a powerful hold over him. On the other hand...

"Quite soon we will come to a good place to stop," he said.

"Lovely," she said. "It is like doing revision for my finals, when I would bribe myself through each chapter with a bar of chocolate at the end. I never sat the exams, but I put on twelve pounds."

She was a lovely woman, plump and strong. She laughed—not a giggle but a deep laugh like a man's—with the pleasure of love. She had suckled children and her breasts were large and soft, but there was a straightforwardness about her caresses and demands that suggested that she had not had many lovers.

"Ah, that is good, that is good," she whispered, rocking him gently to and fro on her in the dusk-filled room.

"It enlarges the soul," he answered.

"I didn't know that," she sighed.

"Yes, it enlarges the soul."

This was an affirmation of truth against the nightmare brutalities of the cellar and the lake, so he spoke the words louder than he need have.

"I believe you," she said.

"Oh, I do not know that it enlarges *women's* souls."

161

She laughed her pleased laugh and pinched his left buttock.

They became like lovers in an idyll, who have been miraculously given leave to break step from the iron march of Time and to follow their own by-ways at their own pace. This was not the dead abstraction of the hours that he had endured in the cellar, but a calendar of their own choosing. It enabled them to do huge stints of solid work, exploring the intricate and infolded valleys of mathematical probability. Then they would make love, then sleep, whatever time the sun declared outside.

Humayan woke once, in the dark, and started to run through the chain of his reasoning, looking for weak links. She must have been awake too, and perhaps heard the alteration of his breathing.

"Relax, Pete, relax," she whispered.

"Oh, I am very relaxed. But I have been thinking about the work we did today. I want to make it as safe as possible for you—I did not care before, you know, but now I want to protect you as much as I can."

She slid her arm under his ribs and clutched him to her like a child with a doll. For the first time he realised how frightened she was of the job she had been singled out for; their work might keep her mind busy, but her lustfulness was a way of appeasing the terrors of her body and her deeper being.

"You need not do it at all," he said. "They can find someone else and I will teach her."

Her hug slackened.

"I have a husband and two sons," she said. "I had not been thinking of telling you of them. My man is a checker at Cardiff Docks, but he is a genius with it—a bard, a song-maker, as good as any of them in a hundred years. Only there's no printing of his songs, by law. They go from hand to hand and from mouth to mouth, without even his name to them. I have heard another man singing in a pub for drinks, singing one of my man's best songs, one that he made for me, and this other man telling all the customers that he wrote it himself, and them knowing no better. He is a bit of a drinker too, my man, but no worse than some. Our two boys are good boys, with good brains, and we teach them all we can, for the schools, you know, are only permitted to teach them enough to make them checkers in docks. Shameful it is. So for them and their kind I must strike a blow—that's one thing. The other is that if I say no, my man will come back from work with his head broken, or there'll be a fire-bomb thrown into the room where my boys sleep—yes, it has happened. It is the innocent who are punished in a war like ours."

Her hand began to slide along his thigh but he caught it and held it still.

"What kind of a people are you?" he said. "How can you do these things to each other and still believe it is a good cause you are fighting in?"

"I have read that at the partition of India refugee trains came into the stations with every passenger dead and blood running from the carriages so that the wheels could not grip the rails."

"It was those Moslem swine," he said angrily.

Her laugh, for once, was a jeer. Then she sighed.

"We are a brutalised people," she said. "We always have been. Perhaps it is something in our blood. The Irish, you know, are more cruel than the Scots, but the Scots are more deliberate in their cruelty. However it is, we are all brutalised. Listen, Pete, the sort of treatment we have had—for centuries we have had it, but always growing worse—that sort of treatment makes it impossible to follow virtue. The straight and narrow path has been blown up, and we are left with a choice of roads to destruction. All choices are evil, but I am sure of one thing; to do nothing, not to fight, to sit in degradation for ever, that is to perpetuate the evil. All possible action is also evil, but good might come of it. I do not say good will come, good *might* come. I choose that possibility, however faint, against the certainty of perpetual degradation."

"Would you throw a bomb into a room where children of your own race slept?"

"No, I cannot conceive of myself doing that. But, Pete, I can understand the mind that does it, and thinks it

163

right to do it. And listen, Pete. Until you have made the effort to understand how it feels to act like that, what it means to be so brutalised, you have no right to judge us. Nobody has any right to judge us."

"As a child I was taught that all action is evil, however well-intended, as binding the soul closer to the wheel of the world."

"That's an easy way out. I do not wonder that the English rulers discouraged the missionaries who tried to wean their subjects from that line of thinking. Oh, Pete, Pete, don't judge us, don't you judge me. That's all."

There was only one other little eddy in the smooth flow of their idyll. One morning Alan came to their room and explained that the brother-in-law of the German Chancellor was coming to see the house, which was kept in exquisite historic nick as proof that the zoning laws did not deprive Greens of cultural equality, though in fact it was only opened for the occasional foreign white VIP. The difficulty was that the previous major-domo, who had been a casualty of the shoot-out, had been a very slight gentleman, and none of the new group could get into his magnificent uniform. So if Humayan would condescend to green up for the occasion...

Anna was reluctant, but Alan produced a press cutting from an American newspaper showing Mr. Zass, with his leg in plaster, shaking hands with the American ambassador in Dublin. So Humayan saw that he would have to show, even at some risk to himself, a similar gesture of goodwill. Anna coached his Indian accent into Welsh, and he spent a morning weighed down with gold braid and unearned medals, which tinkled every time he bowed, as he did at the entrance to each of the magnificent rooms their camera-clicking visitors inspected. The German tipped him five pounds when they left, but Anna would not let him touch her until he had removed the last faint smear of green grease from his skin.

After that the days of lust and cerebration flowed with a glassy impetus towards the cliff of parting.

PART III

Noside

IX

*Thus is it written. Before the Incarnation of the Sid-
dartha (blessed be he) there lived in a northern province
the wisest man in the world. For thirty and three years
had he grown, and for thirty and three years had he
acquired wisdom, and for thirty and three years had he
taught and kings came to him for counsel. And in his
hundredth year he spoke to his disciples, saying, Now will
I meditate. Let none come near me. So for thirty and
three years did he sit in silence beneath a lemon tree
and his disciples tended his body. And in his hundred
and thirty-third year he stirred and looked about him.
Then his disciples spoke to him, saying, Master, may our
ears be blessed with the fruits of thy meditation. And he
answered saying, For three and thirty years I have medi-
tated on this one question, namely whether among the
sands of the desert there be two grains of sand that are in
every way identical. And his disciples said to him, Master,
is this not a small question for thee, who art the wisest
man in the world. And he answered them saying, Per-
adventure it is a small question, but it was too large for
me, and I found no answer.*

"OK," said Mr. Mann in a voice of finality, "if they
aren't going to make a song and dance about it, we
won't either. We'll get a doctor's report out, saying that
you've had a period of amnesia. Shock of seeing Horseman's Yard go up. That OK by you?"

"Are they all dead?" said Humayan.

"Who?"

"The Glisters."

"Yeah. Tough, wasn't it? That Katie was a pretty piece. Wait a minute, there was the other girl who got out, but the blast knocked her cold—yes, hold it, there was something I wanted to clear with you about that. Hang on."

He picked a folder off his desk instead of getting the report from the big machine. So he had been expecting to ask this question, and the last-minute interest was false. He glanced through the papers with a perfunctoriness that confirmed this, then laid them down and tapped a paragraph.

"Here it is," he said. "The girl was holding a dog-collar which she said she'd given you as a joke. It had some writing on the inside. Know anything about that?"

"I hope that did not cause trouble," muttered Humayan, no longer having to *act* obsequiousness. "The joke was that she is a witch, and she made me wear the collar as a symbol of her power over me. I wrote a mantra on the inside, a protection against witches. It was all very silly."

"Ogham?"

"Oh, that is a secret language of this country, so I thought the mantra might have greater power here written like that, you know?"

Mr. Mann stared. For the moment his emotions were naked, as astonishment shaded into contempt.

"Christ!" he said, closing the file.

"I hope I have caused no trouble," gabbled Humayan, who had steeled himself to other areas of lying and was unprepared for this. "I was intrigued by Ogham, you know. The linear element and the counting element have the feeling of a very primitive computer coding, you see..."

"Christ," sighed Mr. Mann, returning to his carapace of bureaucratic efficiency. He picked up a metallic ink pen, altered the coding on the outer slip and fed the documents back into the machine.

"You'd better get back to work," he said. "Don't tell anyone where you've been. We'll book you in to an hotel."

"I have a friend I can stay with."

168

"OK. So long, Pete. Watch your step."

The outer office had changed. Bound volumes of *Prism* stocked the brand-new bookshelves and galley-proofs littered the floor. Several extremely tough-looking filing-cabinets stood against a wall. But Tarquin, just as before, was reading the details of the day's accumulator from his Telex screen into the phone. That was a bonus, Humayan thought.

The work he had been hired to do no longer held his mind, but he forced himself through massive calculations because in the course of them he was able to test many of his assumptions about the total programming of the big machine in the basement. He discovered one danger-point only, and a few minor simplifications besides the big simplification that Tarquin was still in the same office and still betting. He had deliberately bought a morning paper, and that evening he stuffed it into the litter bin ten yards down from Mr. Palati's restaurant; the green street-sweeper scuffling along the gutter towards him did not hurry his pace; but Humayan, talking to Mr. Palati, saw the man take the paper, pretend to glance at the head-lines, and then fold it into his jacket pocket before empty-ing the rest of the bin into his cart.

A few days later Humayan worked till after supper-time and left the building by way of the A corridor. A vacuum-cleaner hummed in A3 so he slipped inside; a green woman was sweeping the floor with careful strokes while Anna dusted the Telex keyboard, frowning. She looked up at him, smiled minutely and nodded. He put the key on the desk beside her, and her fingers touched his as she picked it up. He pointed to the black-and-white abstract that hung where the Oxfam child had been, put his finger to his lips, kissed his hand to her and left. She was stripped and searched whenever she came to the building, so that she would have to find a hiding-place in the office and leave it there. She would choose some-thing clever and sensible, he thought. She was like that. He was very depressed as he made his way home, thinking he would never see her again.

*   *   *

169

This depression deepened over the days. One evening, almost without knowing what he was doing, he took the tube that he had habitually used when he had been living with the Glisters and got out at the same old station. The Avenue seemed unaltered except for being dustier as the urban season swung towards autumn. The leaves on the plane trees were larger, too, and less sappy. But the same gaunt sweeper came up the gutter towards him, nudging his pile of effluvium. The sunk, blood-shot eyes fell for an instant on Humayan, stared for a startled nano-second and swung away. Humayan strolled towards the man.

"Got a light, mister?" he said.

The man muttered and did not look up.

"It is all right," said Humayan. "I told the RRB that I was stunned by the explosion and woke up a prisoner. But in fact my captors did not know why I had been captured, nor on whose orders ... Listen, sir, if you do not tell me I will inform the RRB of the true fact. If you do, I will keep silence. I give you my word."

The man stopped sweeping, straightened up and scratched his head under his cap. His height and melancholy and bafflement gave him the look of a great ape in a zoo, a creature so far out of its natural element that it can do nothing but stare at the passing crowds with an air of tragic bewilderment.

"It wasna canny," he muttered. "Five green shentlemen I hadna kent before cam tae tak up my paving, and ain of them spak wi me and askit after ye, and when wad yoursel be passing. And ye didna come and ye didna come, and syne they gan filling in their hole agin, but they didna fill it a'; and yon mon wha had askit me callit me over and gave me a wee claith to pit ower your face, and said that I was tae pick ye up if I could, and tak ye to a hoose he told me of. Sae I pickit ye up, but I didna mind the address o yon hoose, sae I carried ye awa tae the gang I kent, and they took ye awa. But they kent naething aboot ye, and nae mair of the ither gang. Mon, but they were sair fashed that a kidnapping could be plannit in their ain territory, and themselves nae kenning ocht aboot it."

He laughed suddenly at the anger of his friends, a sour and melancholy sound. Humayan gave him a florin, and left him still shaking his head at the strangeness of things.

The pub was not yet open. The alley that led to Horseman's Yard was half blocked by the scaffolding from which the builders were repairing the bomb-damage to the pub, but the workmen had gone home so Humayan ducked through.

The iron gates were gone, and so was everything else. Where the Sunday morning sherry-glasses had twinkled was a scree of rubble. The Glisters' house, Mr. Leary's and the other house that side were completely collapsed; those on the other sides of the yard had not a window between them; a vast green tarpaulin covered a hole in the gymnasium roof. Among the jumbled bricks odd fragments of belongings poked out—shards of bright pottery that had once been lampstands, gilded slivers of wood that had framed garish abstracts or paintings of African elephants. Elsewhere, perhaps as part of the process of getting the bodies out, a vague attempt at tidying up had been begun and then abandoned, so that piles of brick had been roughly stacked together into ugly pyramids and splintered floorboards tossed into a heap. Humayan picked his way over to another such pile, which was simply a miscellany of bric-à-brac, and looked up at the gymnasium wall. Hovering invisible up there was the ghost of a bed on which happy, pretty Kate Glister had had her pleasure; and a few yards to its left the ghost of a spyhole through which no draught would any longer whistle. His eye began to water and his other eye wept with it. He looked down at the junk at his feet and through the mists of grief discerned a small brass object, twinkling.

He stooped and plucked it out of the mess, and the leather strap came with it. The word on the tag was 'Ought'. When he had cleaned the collar with his handkerchief and buckled it round his left wrist he found it meant nothing at all. He turned away uncomforted.

She was waiting for him at the pillar-box on the corner

of the main road. He thought it was a tramp or beggar-woman, especially when she came hobbling towards him with one beseeching hand outstretched, as if for money. Indians learn in early childhood how to ignore beggars, but now he was taken unawares.

"Pete," she said. "Pete. Don't go away, please!"

He swallowed with shock. Before he could recognise her for sure she staggered against him and buried her head on his shoulder. She stank.

"Where have you been?" he said.

"In prison. They let me out a week ago ... I hadn't anywhere to go. I hadn't got any money. I didn't know what had happened to the Yard. Helen's parents wouldn't let her talk to me. The school ... I've been living out of dustbins like ... like a Green."

He had not believed, when he had known her before, that he would ever hear her cry. She did not do so easily. Her sobs were wrenched through the torn shell of her confidence, each one an agony. There seemed to be nothing that would help her stop.

Up the avenue, under the planes, floated a yellow light. Humayan pushed himself free and ran to the kerb, waving. She clung to his sleeve saying, "Don't leave me! Don't leave me!" The taxi stopped but the green driver looked with distrust at his prospective fares, a small brown man and a battered female who might be any colour. He slid the gear-lever forward.

"I will pay double, double!" shrieked Humayan.

"Double double is four times, mister," said the cabbie.

"All right," said Humayan. The green grin was malicious but the green hand put the flag down. Humayan had to help Glenda up the step; she was still sobbing when she collapsed on to the worn leather of the seat. Humayan gave the address of Mr. Palati's restaurant and when they reached it paid the quadruple fare but refused to add a tip. The man drove off with neither curse nor thanks.

It was too early for supper customers. Mr. Palati was sitting at the window table faking his accounts with one hand and drinking tea with the other.

"Good evening, good evening," he said. "Oh, the lady

has trouble. Shall I telephone the hospital, Pravi?"

"No, no," whispered Glenda. "I want to stay with you."

"Sirri, my friend," said Humayan earnestly, "you must trust me. I will explain it all later. Now this poor girl must wash and rest and eat, and there is nowhere but my room. No, it is not what you think, Sirri—look at her. I knew her father."

"Ah," said Mr. Palati, beaming out of his doubt. "The debt to a parent is a debt that must be paid. Mine are long dead, thank the gods. Shall I make you a tray to take up?"

"Oh you are a good man, Sirri, a very good man. Not a strong curry, you understand."

Mr. Palati beamed. His little black eyes glittered in the fat folds of his cheeks at the sudden excitement and mystery and scandal. Humayan led Glenda out past the heavy reek of the kitchen and the milder, sourer odour from the lavatories to the lino-covered staircase. His shock and horror were ebbing from him now, and as he heaved Glenda up the last flight he became almost gigglish with the thought that it was a mercy he had never met Selina under such circumstances. This notion was no doubt started by the décor with which Mr. Palati signalled the difference between his public and private lives—downstairs and on the first floor wallpaper and curtains were all of an irreducible prudish dinginess, but up here every free surface was covered with enormous erotic posters for which Mr. Palati had made a special trip to Denmark.

Glenda appeared not even to notice them. She staggered through the door which Humayan held open for her, collapsed on the bed and started to sob again, but more easily now. Humayan fetched a jug of warm water from the bathroom and sponged her face, but before he had finished there was a knock on the door. Mr. Palati beckoned him out.

"I have some ladies' clothes in a cupboard," he whispered. "It is a little hobby of mine."

He took Humayan along to the locked door which shut off the far end of the corridor, opened it and led the way through.

"You will not laugh at me?" he whispered.

The suite was furnished like rooms in a Bombay romantic film, all mirrors and pink gauze and twinkling knick-knacks and ostrich-feathers and buttoned stools bulging with stuffing and a vast, circular bed. Mr. Palati slid open the doors of a fitted cupboard and revealed an array of astounding dresses.

"Three sizes I have," he said with shy pride. "You see, several ladies come, and they dress up to amuse me."

He ran a dark hand caressingly down what appeared to be a cutaway track suit of soft black leather. Then he smiled his giggling smile and tiptoed back to his currys.

Glenda was lying on the bed, feebly trying to wipe her spectacles one-handed on the pillowcase. Humayan quickly looked away from her unguarded gaze.

"These bloody things," she said. "They get so filthy when I cry. Is there a bath, Pete?"

"Yes indeed, yes indeed. And my friend Mr. Palati has some clean clothes too. But I'm afraid ... well, you must see."

He left her pawing, too feeble for hysterics, at the Palati Collection. Twenty minutes later, when he came into his room with a tray of food, she was sitting on the edge of the bed draped in a blue sari which he had not noticed. She was wearing it all wrong but only allowed him to make minor adjustments.

"I'm not wearing anything else," she said. "You'll have to burn all my clothes, Pete. He's got some smashing underclothes there, but ... and in any case I wouldn't be able to do the bra. Something's happened to my left arm, so it won't do what I tell it."

He put the tray on his chair so that she could reach it from the bed, and himself settled cross-legged on the floor. She took a long time to finish the small helping which he had purposely brought her, knowing the ways of starvation.

"We had curried chicken in your room once," she said as she put her fork down. "Your ... other room, I mean."

"Why did they put you in prison?" he asked. He knew the answer, but wanted to know whether she knew, and why she had been so mistreated.

"It was something to do with Daddy," she said. "At first I couldn't understand anything, but then from the questions they asked I worked out that he was some sort of ... I don't know."

"He was in charge of a department called R5, which is involved in secret work overseas."

"Yes, something like that. Some days they were quite nice, and some days ... oh, there was a man with cricket bats on his tie and very short hair. It was always a bad day then. He seemed to think that I'd joined the Greens, joined them against Daddy ... oh, Pete, that collar. It was written on in Ogham. That's what they kept coming back to. Pete, did *you* write that stuff?"

He nodded.

"But what was it? What was it? That worried me more than anything. I used to think if only I knew that I wouldn't mind what else they did."

"A charm against witches."

Now she was strong enough for hysterics. He snatched the tray away before she could upset it, then stood over her watching the working muscles of her face and listening to the unstoppable, shrill, agonised whooping—that noise, as of a dog wailing at the end of its chain, which the soul makes as it tries to burst itself free from the intolerable kennel of flesh. In the end he nerved himself to slap her but had to pluck the spectacles clear first. At the touch of his fingers the noise stopped. She seemed to try to shrink down into the bed, whispering words he could not hear. In twenty seconds she was asleep.

She was still asleep next morning when he woke all stiff with sleeping on a borrowed mattress on the floor.

"Sirri, my friend," he said to Mr. Palati, "you will look after the girl? I will tell you—I stayed in the house of her father when I came to England. And then the Greens bombed it and all her family were killed. I lost my memory, as I have told you, and went wandering about, but the police thought that this girl had helped with the bomb, killing her own family. They thought this because of something I had given her, and they were very cruel to her. Now they have let her go and I have found her. She has done nothing. It was all a mistake—my

175

stupidity—she is quite innocent."

Mr. Palati's heavy but normally happy face clouded at the mention of the police and did not clear again.

"This restaurant is my life, Pravi," he said. "Already I pay protection to the police—you know they could put a bomb in here and say the Greens did it. They are swine. I cannot anger them."

Humayan drew his National Insurance Card from his wallet and slid it across the cash-desk.

"That is my hostage," he said. "You keep that, and I will return this evening with a residence permit for the girl."

They shook hands over the deal, very solemnly.

"You are a good man, Sirri," said Humayan. "I think you are the only good man I have ever met."

Mr. Palati looked at him in astonishment.

"That is not what my ladies say," he chuckled. "Very much not."

Humayan left him beaming with the remembered pleasure of what his ladies had said to him and what had caused them to say it.

To know your way round an organisation is one thing. To know your way through it is another. In the time since he had returned from captivity Humayan had begun to learn the latter art, and though he was by no means an adept he had discovered one or two tunnellings of which Mr. Mann was only dimly aware. He got Glenda's card and residence permit from an apparently very lowly official; they cost him twenty-eight pounds. The clerk generously threw into the bargain a coding which Humayan chose, partly because it could have no connection with the family that had lived in Horseman's Yard.

"In any case the big machine's got gremlins," he said. "So if there's any kick-back we can put it down to that."

He peeled his chewing-gum off the tiny grid of the concealed microphone by his desk and changed the subject to that which Humayan had ostensibly come to visit him about.

Mr. Palati returned the Insurance Card with a flourish

and did not even ask to see Glenda's documents.

"I have put a bed in the little room opposite yours, Pravi," he said. "It is not pretty, but you must have two rooms. This is a most respectable house. That is what I am always telling my ladies."

He laughed until the drawer of the cash register shot open with the vibrations and nudged him in the stomach.

Glenda woke to the rattle of the cutlery on the tray. At first she tried to worm herself further into the bed, but then her head poked clear.

"We've only just had supper," she said in a complaining voice. "But don't take it away. I'm still hungry."

For the next week Humayan worked with real verve and interest at the new task he had set himself, though odd little things—the intonation of a colleague, the length of time the switchboard operator took over his calls, the chilliness of his morning coffee—told him that he was not any longer the brightest hope of the organisation. He didn't mind. As he said to Glenda one evening, "You see they all despise me. It is only partly a race thing. They have decided that I am—what was Kate's word?—a creep. Yes, I am a creep, it is true. But I am not a creep all through. That is where they make their mistake, because they despise everything I do, and forget that in one way I am better than any of them. In one way I am Mr. Muscles. I will outwit them. I will destroy Mr. Mann."

"Who's he?" said Glenda in the leaden tones she used all the time.

"A man with cricket bats on his tie and short hair. He hated your father. He was glad of the excuse to torture you."

"Oh."

Even this information failed to make any impact on the dullness of her desolation. But she had evidently taken it in, for when he was settling her down for the night she said, "Don't bother about that man with the cricket bats, Pete. Don't bother. It doesn't matter. It's just something that happened, like a traffic accident."

Once more he was alarmed at her powers, her ability to see into his mind, her knowledge that he intended to bother.

Next Saturday morning he used his RRB pass to wander up into the Zone. Action, as Anna had said, is sometimes necessary even against hopeless odds, because the odds against inaction lie at that infinity where the hyperbole meets the axis. He had vague ideas of actually stopping strangers and questioning them, but having been stopped and questioned himself by policemen a couple of times he no longer had the nerve. He wandered in an almost dreamy mood through the hot, littered streets, where the chief activities seemed to be mending very old cars and leaning against rusty railings. A few of last night's drunks still lay on the pavements. Only the children seemed to move and speak as though there were any luck to be had out of this world. The shops here were small and solitary, their windows obscured by old advertisements for pipe-tobacco and sewing machines.

Humayan zigzagged to and fro until he was lost. Then he paused and stared at a pawnbroker's shop. The window, which had a grille over it, contained watches and jewellery, but the customers went in empty-handed and emerged with several suits of clothing over their arms. Humayan watched a plumpish, plainish girl strut into the shop on shoes whose soles were so thick and heels so high that they made her appear four inches taller than she was. He had always resented the fact that it was not ridiculous for a woman to add to her stature in such a fashion, but when he had tried it all his cousins, and even some of his aunts, had giggled all day. He gazed after the girl with dislike.

An argument rose inside the shop, a man's voice against a woman's. The girl emerged, flushed and pouting, with the usual set of male suitings draped over her arm. A bald man in shirtsleeves followed her out, brandishing another garment.

"Would I have taken it in if ye'd told me you wasn't going to redeem it pay-days?" he snarled.

The girl strutted away without answering.

"What good is it to me?" he shouted, brandishing the garment to the street, so that all the gold glittered on its lapels.

"Take up amateur thayatricals, uncle," shouted a railing-leaner.

Humayan moved away. The girl was easy to follow, because of her walk. Her skirt was so short that folds of her buttocks showed like jowls above her green thighs. At first he sneaked along, but then he realised that if she disappeared into a house he would have the fresh problem of making contact, so he hurried his pace and caught her on the very steps. They led down to a stinking basement area.

"Miss, miss," he whispered.

She turned and stared through the railing at him, sulky-eyed.

"I want to see Frank," he whispered.

Her face closed and hardened.

"Tell him it's Pete," he said. "Just tell him what I look like."

She turned without word or sign and teetered down the ragged steps. Humayan waited, leaning against the railings like a native. After five minutes the door below opened and she hissed at him to come down. Her eyes held a speculative look now, but she said nothing as she led him along a passage full of bicycles and pointed to a dark brown door. He knocked. A known tone grunted. He went in.

It was a woman's room, full of cheap odours and holy knick-knacks. Mr. Leary lay on the bed, wearing a pair of pyjamas far too small for him. His face, from long hiding, had the colour and texture of concrete from which the shuttering has just been stripped.

"Hi," he said. "Didn't expect to see you here. How did you find me?"

Humayan told him.

"That bitch," said Mr. Leary. "Christ, she's stupid. Can you lend me the cash to get it out of hock, old man? Even a thick-headed copper might make the connection. The going rate for a coat's two quid in these parts."

179

Humayan counted five pound notes on to the dresser.
"How are you?" he said.

"Burnt out," said Mr. Leary. "Shell-shocked. It's like metal fatigue. You stand the stresses OK for years, so you think you'll stand them for ever. Then you snap, under no load at all. I'd like to get out of the country, but none of them will handle me. I'm starting to wish those apes had shot me. You won't believe this, old man, but I can't stop thinking about Katie. Jesus, I was a fool about that."

His voice, which had been a model of half-humorous resignation at the beginning of this speech, was now tinged with soft self-pity.

"That is what I came to ask you about," said Humayan stiffly. Mr. Leary's eyes half closed, but as he turned his head away his pupils remained fixed on Humayan.

"Let me explain," said Humayan. "Moirag had tried to poison me, and Mr. Mann learnt of this. Before I left for home that evening he told me that Moirag was now fixed. A kidnap gang, unconnected with the local organisation, attempted to waylay me before I reached Horseman's Yard. Mr. Mann had asked when I was going home. You were one of his agents. What I need to know is whether Mr. Mann knew that you were intending to blow up the Glisters' house."

"Go and chase a rabbit," said Mr. Leary.

Humayan shrugged. He had several possible levers, including the simple threat to betray the man on the bed, but he thought it would be demeaning to employ them.

"I will give you ten pounds for an honest answer," he said calmly.

"Fifty," said Mr. Leary.

"Twenty," said Humayan. He put the two notes with the others on the dresser and shut his wallet with a snap. His back pay had accumulated beautifully while he had been living cheaply as a prisoner, but there was no point in wasting it on this trash. Mr. Leary sighed.

"OK," he said. "I didn't get precise orders, but I knew what he wanted, and he knew I knew. Only he didn't know it suited me. That's all."

"But he watched Glenda being tortured," protested Humayan.

Mr. Leary made an enquiring grumble. Humayan explained.

"Sure," said Mr. Leary. "He'd have to go through with that. He couldn't let on how he knew she'd had nothing to do with it, could he? That's an organisation where half your colleagues go about with a permanent crouch, just in case they get the chance to snatch the rug from under you."

"I see," said Humayan. He stood for a moment looking at the money on the dresser. He would have liked to take the five pounds back so that he could redeem the coat and send it to Mr. Zass, but that would have been an extra risk.

"Thank you," he said suddenly. "Goodbye."

Mr. Leary started on a sentence of protest, but then sighed, waved a dismissive hand and lay back on the bed.

The girl was waiting in the passageway. She beckoned Humayan up to the further end, then whispered, "Will you be turning him in, mister? Will I be getting the reward?"

Humayan looked up at her, which he would not have needed to do had she been wearing more decorous shoes.

"I would prefer him to stay here," he said. "What rent is he paying you?"

"Him!" she sneered.

"All right. I will pay you five pounds a week, in advance, provided he stays here. You understand?"

"Ach, I can keep him," she answered with a curiously repulsive movement of her torso, a small free sample of what she regarded as her allure. "It will be a change having a man in the house who's bringing the money in."

Humayan nodded. They understood each other very well. As he turned the corner of the street he made sure that he remembered its name.

The women in the enquiry office of R14 were just as polite as before, but more distant. Also he had to wait long enough to read three whole copies of *Prism* before

Mr. Mann was free to see him, though he had come punctually for his appointment. But Mr. Mann himself was quite unchanged.

"Sorry to keep you, Pete," he said. "Some sod's been mucking about with the big machine—you had any trouble?"

"A little. I have taken to running my programmes two ways. You have got a rat there."

"A what?"

"An electronic rat. You sometimes get them in big machines. It is only a way of saying it, but they are hard to catch, like real rats."

"I'm beginning to think we've got a human rat somewhere," said Mr. Mann. "Sit down. What's the matter? You look nervous."

"I am nervous," said Humayan truthfully. "I will tell you. While I was a prisoner I had nothing to do but think. It stopped me from being so frightened. I thought about the work I had been doing here and I came to certain conclusions. I did not tell you about them at first because even I cannot do the necessary calculations in my head. Since I came back I have been checking them through. It will be a long time before I can publish any scientifically acceptable results, but already I can see with reasonable certainty which way my work is leading, and I am afraid you will not like it."

"Don't mind me," said Mr. Mann, reaching for the tape-recorder switch.

"The results fall into two separate but linked sets," said Humayan. "First, the probabilities are that this country is due for another surge in the green population in the very near future."

"That's not too bad. We can cope with that provided we know about it."

"Perhaps. But after a very complex but perfectly valid series of calculations I am getting a significant correlation with another factor which we had not considered before. The intensity of the surge will be proportional to the severity of the ... er, discipline ... or restriction ... what they would call repression ... experienced by the Celts."

"What the hell do you mean by that?"

"Put it this way. There are a lot of variables, but I have taken as many of the measurable factors as I can find—things like freedom of movement and income in real terms and life-expectancy and so on. There is going to be a surge in any case, but if you do not wish to see, in one generation, a minority of Saxons living among a majority of green Celts, then you must either wipe the Celts out altogether or you must dramatically relax the restrictions that now exist. And certainly any attempt to control the coming surge by more repressive measures will have the opposite effect. This is not as surprising as it seems. I have been reading a Ministry of Agriculture pamphlet on the control of pigeons..."

"Bugger pigeons," said Mr. Mann, pressing a buzzer.

"Your slave to command," said the ceiling.

"Cut that out," said Mr. Mann. "Get Pollock over here at once. Put a gun at his head if he won't come. Cancel everything for me..."

"The Home Sec..." protested the ceiling.

"Cancel him," said Mr. Mann and switched the switch off.

By now Humayan was having to make a deliberate effort to appear more nervous than he felt. He knew Professor Pollock's work, which was clumsy and old-fashioned. Pollock, even if he went over and commandeered the Treasury computer, would take at least a month to discover the mistakes which Humayan had built in to his calculations and then buried layers deep.

"Right," said Mr. Mann. "Got anything on paper?"

Humayan slid across the desk the twenty folio sheets he had prepared. Mr. Mann began to read them, looked at the lace-work of equations and pushed them aside.

"Kept a copy?" he said.

"I have one for myself and there is one in the Indian High Commission."

"Why the hell?"

"Oh, you will think it silly, but I am a very nervous man and I have been through a frightening time. I can see this information would be extremely, er, inconvenient for you if it were generally known before you are ready for it. And I know you for a practical fellow, Mr. Mann.

You would think it right to prevent this information from being published. You would take drastic steps."

Mr. Mann looked at him steadily. After the first flicker of surprise his stare was unreadable.

"OK," he said at last, acknowledging nothing but simply accepting the situation as it was, "what do you want?"

"It is difficult for me," said Humayan with earnest humility. "My family, they see their genius go off to England, to a fine job. They expect great things. They are very ambitious for me, especially my uncle Prim. All I want, Mr. Mann, is to leave, to go away quietly with my girl-friend."

"No can do."

"Oh, I see your difficulty, I assure you. You think I will take my work to America or somewhere. These findings..." he waved casually at the sheaf of calculations, "they would be very popular in some universities. They have a *political* significance, you know? Of course I understand you cannot permit that."

"You haven't told me why you want to go."

"Oh, I am sorry, but I do not like it here. I am a timid chap. These bombings, these kidnappings. And you know, I am not racially suited to the climate of this culture of yours. I am pining away. I must go to India, as soon as possible. My documents tell a lie. I am not a Saxon."

"Uh-huh. What's your offer?"

"I leave you my work. Any truly competent expert can follow it up. I guarantee to do no more work on the green gene, nor to refer again either in public or in private to the work I have done. Oh, I know you have a long arm, Mr. Mann. You will find a way to punish me if I break my guarantee."

"Yeah."

"Of course I arrange for the Indian High Commission to return you that copy as soon as I am out of the country. I will give you mine today. That is my side of the bargain. In return you will give me two air tickets to India, a year's severance pay, a top-rate reference saying how satisfied you are with my work, and an exit visa for my girl-friend."

"She white?"

"I am afraid so."

Mr. Mann looked at him for some time, his thoughts completely masked.

"What's her coding?" he said at last.

Humayan's fingers barely shook as he passed across the little slip on which the numbers were written. Mr. Mann tapped them out on his console, then leaned back in his chair to gaze in silence at the ceiling until the machine did its fizz and click and the little plastic rectangle shot across the desk. He picked up, then threw it across the room with a shout of rage. Humayan went and retrieved it. The photograph was of Mr. Mann, and the biographical details consisted of nothing but his name, coding and date of birth.

"Please wait," said Humayan as Mr. Mann reached for the telephone. "I think perhaps I have found your rat for you."

"Huh?"

Humayan pretended to study the card for twenty seconds. Then he did the same with Glenda's number.

"Yes, yes," he sighed. "That might be it. There is a considerable coincidence between these numbers in binary notation. Let me see..."

He thought for an instant and wrote a new number below Glenda's.

"Send for that, sir," he said. "I do not know whose coding it is, but I think we will get your card again."

And so, of course, it proved.

"Well, that's something," said Mr. Mann heavily. "How the hell d'you think it happened?"

"Oh, any number of ways. Somebody—some amateur —using the machine for his own purposes without consulting a systems analyst. He sets up the coincidence by accident, and by accident instructs it to destroy the original instruction and reinstruct itself afresh. Shall I talk to your computer men?"

Mr. Mann nodded, dialled three numbers, spoke briefly and passed the telephone over. The man at the other end understood at once, and started calling across the room to his colleagues with a huntsman's cries of excitement. Humayan added a small extra clue and put the receiver down.

"Christ, I'll be glad to have the machine going OK again," said Mr. Mann. "OK, I'm going to buy your package, Pete."

"Thank you."

"You can cut that out. I don't like to be blackmailed, and it doesn't happen often, but I've got a feeling you're trouble. I got where I am by listening to that sort of feeling. So I want you out of the country, pronto. Pollock can check this stuff through with you for a couple of days, and you can fly Friday. This girl got a passport?"

"I don't think so."

"OK, I'll have a registrar out at the airport and you can marry her there. She can go on yours. That'll make her an Indian citizen. I'm not having her back."

To be forcibly wedded to a witch!

"You are most kind," said Humayan.

"Cut that out. Now..."

They discussed for five minutes the details of sending the severance pay to Humayan's mother. Mr. Mann took the last note and looked at the ceiling.

"Got Pollock yet?" he said.

"No dice," said the ceiling.

"OK, Pete. Wait over there. You'll find a few magazines."

Humayan sat in a too-cosy chair and looked at an old copy of *Prism*. It contained a scholarly article by Gideon Glister on the folk-rites of Liverpool dockers. Humayan had already read that, in far-away Bombay. He turned to the small ads and found his own advertisement. It meant nothing. But studying the neighbouring snippets he thought he could begin to detect traces of a code by which a man sitting in an office in London could instruct foreign agents. No wonder the editor had written them all himself.

"We've got Pollock," said the ceiling suddenly. "He's in a tizz—he was having some morning massage from a fat girl at the Daffodil. He'll be along in an hour."

"OK," said Mr. Mann.

"Listen, boss," said the ceiling. "I've got trouble of

186

my own. There's been a maniac on the line from the computer room saying what have I been playing at. I mean, all I've done is use the machine to play the horses a bit, but he says..."

"Christ," said Mr. Mann. "If it was you I'll have your editorial balls. OK, Pete. Be around in an hour. I'll send Pollock up to your office. Watch your step."

"I must thank you for your help," said Humayan. "And I would like to say goodbye to the Director, if I may."

"Oh, the Old Man says a lovely goodbye," said Mr. Mann dismissively. "He's always got time for that. Ring his secretary and fix it. Her name's Lil."

Professor Pollock was a very handsome old man indeed—the sort of academic who owes his steady promotion to looking the part. Humayan spent some enjoyable vengeful hours throwing invisible dust into his eyes. He was, mercifully, bored by the task he had been set, and would not apply his mind to it with more energy than he needed to follow Humayan's deferential explanations.

The interview with the Director took place next afternoon. Humayan was sick with nerves, but fortunately the Director's palms were permanently clammy so the extra sweatiness of the handshake was not apparent. The noble eyebrows twitched benignly.

"Leaving us to get married, I hear?" said the Director.

"Yes, sir. It is partly that, and partly I fear that my nerves are not good after my kidnapping."

"Ah yes, a very unfortunate business. But we will lay the scoundrels by the heels. I do trust, Mr. Humayan, that apart from that you have enjoyed your visit to our country."

"Oh, yes, sir. All my life I will remember it. I have even enjoyed the food."

The Director answered as if Humayan himself had written the script.

"Have you? Now I like a good curry myself."

"Then you must visit my friend Mr. Palati," said Humayan, opening his briefcase. "His cooking is most

187

authentic. Look, I have a menu here, because of some notes I made for my work during a meal."

He passed the gaudy card across and the Director took it with a slight shrug of embarrassment. Humayan was visibly shuddering as he waited for him to open it. At last he did. The eyebrows shot up, then contracted. Humayan knew the exact words the Director was reading.

SIR, I have heard some rumours of which you ought to know more. I dare not speak aloud of this, for there are hidden microphones in your room. What I have heard is that in the near future the trouble in the big computer will be traced to the young gentleman in A3, and will be made out to be deliberate sabotage. His friendship with you may then be used to unseat you from your position. However, I have also learnt that the man responsible for the assassination of Doctor Glister is hiding at 43 Aboukir Road, W.9, in the basement. I believe this to be known to Department R14, but they are concealing his presence for their own reasons. If he were questioned, he would reveal facts about the explosion at Horseman's Yard which would enable you to counter the threat to yourself. Do not trust anyone in this building.

The Director glanced sideways at Humayan without moving his head.

"Some of this looks pretty indigestible," he said.

"Oh, no, I assure you it is all very good."

"I'm not sure I oughtn't to ask you to stay and help me choose."

This was the next danger point.

"So sorry," said Humayan. "I cannot stay. Mr. Mann has made very kind arrangements to fly me out in haste. And I am sure you know more about Indian food than I do. I am not a great expert."

The Director stared long at the garish card, as if unable to make up his mind between Methee Bhaji and Duck Vindaloo. The point was that he was in no position to challenge a powerful and entrenched official such as Mr. Mann without careful preparation. To him it must appear that Humayan's hasty dispatch was part of the plot, and to interfere with that would be to put Mr. Mann on his guard. Evidently the Director followed this train of reasoning without further prompting.

"Well," he said, "it has been an honour to have you working for us, Mr. Humayan. I'm sure we will all remember you for a long time."

"Oh, I hope so," said Humayan with a sudden rush of pleasure at being allowed to tell the exact truth.

He was searched, quite politely, as he left the building, but he had expected this and carried nothing more than the usual detritus from a cleared desk. It was going to be an agony to wait the fourteen hours until they were safely on the plane. So many things could happen. Mr. Mann or the Director could change their minds, Anna make a mistake, Professor Pollock pass on the calculations to some unknown genius of a student. He would have liked to visit a brothel but dared not leave Glenda alone too long. Her unshakeable leaden depression was beginning to frighten him.

On his way home he retired to a public lavatory and wrote a careful note for Anna about how he had hurried the rat-hunt as far as Tarquin, and how rapidly the situation would explode when it reached A_3. The memory of Anna, and her fears, and how she had chosen to assuage them, all mixed themselves up with his worries for Glenda. He wrapped the note in his newspaper, left the lavatory and bought an eye-patch at a chemist's. He was irritated by his own reaction to Glenda. He felt no special affection for her but she was his responsibility, perhaps for the rest of his days. As he squared his moral shoulders for the task he found that he did not even feel particularly noble about taking it on. It was just something that had happened to him, as she said, like a traffic accident. Perhaps it was lucky that Mr. Mann was forcing them into marriage.

She sat on the edge of her bed, gawky and bedraggled, rocking herself to and fro with a motion that suggested that if he didn't stop it now it would go on for ever. He had intended to let them have supper first, but he changed his mind, took the eye-patch out of his pocket and, looking well away from her, plucked her spectacles from her face.

"What the hell?" she said.

Fumblingly, not daring to focus, he adjusted the eye-patch so that it covered her left eye, the eye of the witch; then he could look at her. He did so with compassion, mainly for himself. She was ugly by the standards of any nation. She would never learn to wear a sari. She was a distressing object. He moved and sat beside her and slid his hand round her shoulders so that he could stroke the flesh of her bare right arm. The flesh seemed to contract into chilly rubber under his touch.

"Pete," she croaked.

"I love you," he lied.

"Pete ... what do your friends call you? Mr. Palati calls you something else—not all that stuff you taught me."

"He calls me Pravi."

"Oh. Yes. Well, I suppose that'll do. It'll take a bit of getting used to, Pravi. OK, may I call you Pravi?"

"Of course."

"Oh, Pete, I'm never going to be any use to you. I'm ugly, and I'm clumsy, and I hate being touched, even."

He took his arm away but sat where he was. She was not, after all, a person whom it was proper to lie to.

"It is true that you are not physically attractive," he said. "Not yet—perhaps it will come. But I want to help you. I want to love you. We will wait."

"P ... Pravi, when they were questioning me ... they ... you know it was interesting in a way, just like doctors with a disease that they can't cure. I couldn't tell them anything, and I don't think they specially enjoyed doing it. It was their job. It was a tiresome job, but it was only tiresome because they didn't get results. They were like plumbers come about the central heating. You know, they'd try something, and that didn't work, so they'd just sigh and try something else. So they found out ... oh, I didn't really mind the noises and the dark and all the modern inventions, so they just went back to hurting me, and their way of hurting was ... Oh, Pete, I don't think I'll ever be any use to ... to *anybody*. You'll have to find yourself another girl. Lots of other girls. I won't mind, I promise ... Oh, God, I wish I could stop thinking about Kate."

He took her hand to pat it, but she gripped his fingers convulsively and wouldn't let go. He thought of Mr. Mann, with the cricket bats on his tie, walking towards the trap he had laid for him. He wondered whether there was anything else he could have done to make more sure that Mr. Mann himself would come into the hands of those doctors, those plumbers, who would sigh and try something else. But that was a secondary consideration. Humayan's horoscope said that he was born to be a healer. A man who heals one person is a healer. In that one person he may fulfil his destiny.

"We are going away," he said. "Away from this horrible country."

"But they'll never give me a passport. I've been in prison."

"That is all fixed. Tomorrow we are to be married at the airport, so you will be on my passport. I have the permits and the tickets. I hope you do not object."

She tilted her head over the other way and considered him.

"Poor Pete," she said. "Pravi I mean. Will I like India? Will your mother mind?"

He was pleased by her grasp of essentials.

"You have been in this room all day?" he asked.

"Except to go to the loo."

"Good. You were not disturbed?"

"What do you mean?"

He cupped a theatrical hand behind one ear and pointed to the ceiling. She frowned and shook her head. How they despised him! Not even to bug his girl's room!

"We will not go to India," he said. "I must hide for a little, because things will happen at the RRB and then they may come looking for me. We will leave the flight at Rome, and then I think go to South America. Anyway, somewhere where people do not understand us—where they understand us so little that they do not even believe they understand us."

"That'd be great. There'll have to be a university or something, for you to get a job."

"No good. If they look for me, they will start at universities."

"But what will we live on?"

"Oh, don't you bother about that. I have still some of my back pay, enough for tickets and all that. We will travel in a cheap steamer, and when we get there we will be an astounding team. You will read my mind. We will do astonishing tricks with numbers—very simple —I will teach you. I will perform miracles of memory. Oh yes, even if they discover how we do it they will still be astonished at our cleverness. South Americans are a naïve people."

She fidgeted with the elastic of her eye-patch and looked at him with her head cocked slightly to one side, a mannerism inherited from her mother. At the moment it made her look like a sick crow, bedraggled and weary, but less sick than it had been yesterday, so that now it was ready to consider the acceptance of a crumb. He was worrying about whether Mr. Mann might have ordered a bomb to be placed on their aircraft (it could be blamed on the Greens) and so whether it was worth the extra fuss and delays to ring the airport anonymously and warn them, when she spoke.

"I'll wear gauzy green and a veil. Silver eyelids. Nobody'll mind about my squint if I have silver eyelids. And I'll talk in a voice like *this*. We can get someone on the boat to teach us Spanish and it'll be all right about the accents because magicians ought to sound foreign. But we'll have to have a brilliant name, P-Pravi. You aren't anything if you haven't got a name."

"The Great Minus One?"

"It's a start, anyway."